Loan Wolf

By Harlowe Frost

Printed in the United States of America: First Printing, 2023.

ISBN: 978-1-959981-16-9 (eBook)
ISBN: 978-1-959981-15-2 (paperback)

http://www.hannahwillow217.com

Copy/Line Editor: Angela Grimes
Editor: Weslee Imrisek
Formatting: Huckleberry Rahr
Cover Art: Getcovers.com

Content Warning:

This book contains consensual **BDSM**.

- Tie down
- Blind fold
- Punishment
- Toys

Chapter 1 - I'd Marry Ya
Bexlee

The living room buzzed with the voices of her pack. Bexlee sat in a corner chair reading over the case reports on her tablet. She'd been on the job a week and wanted to catch up with a case that had been ongoing for a few weeks. She could go up to her room, but she felt recharged from the crazy energy everyone gave off.

"But Dad, I want to be a mushroom for Halloween." Five-year-old Stewart stood in the center of the room, feet wide, hands on his hips, face scrunched up in determination. Toys lay scattered around him.

Rainy, at six years old, patiently sat putting together a Lego castle. "I'm going to be a pirate. You could be a princess."

Stewart turned his glare on her then turned to his dad. "Dad, I want to be a mushroom princess for Halloween!" He stomped his foot for emphasis.

Bexlee snorted before scanning through the report to the next section. The case involved a fellow pack mate who was wrapped up in a bigger mess, this case was connected to several others. Of course, no one on the force realized that she knew any of the suspects, and Bexlee wouldn't let that affect her professionalism.

The file was closed, but it was one of four that Cyrus believed was the start of a pattern. It was about a college co-ed named Payton who had died in the arboretum adjacent to the school. They died of an apparent heart attack, though they were young and healthy. Their family didn't have any history of heart problems.

"Are you sure you want to be a princess, Stew? Would you want to wear a dress?" Toby, my brother, asked his son.

"He could wear one of my old dresses; they'd fit him. I have a blue dress with mushrooms and dinosaurs on it." Rainy sat with her knees up, nose in the Lego instruction, trying to figure out the next step of her project.

You'd never know she followed the Halloween costume drama. Bexlee sipped her coffee smiling at the young girl.

Stewart's head snapped to her and then back to Toby. "That's what I want. I want that dress, and a mushroom hat, and red boots. Can that be my costume, Dad? Please?"

Easton, one of their dads, chuckled. Dylan, their other dad, sitting next to him, leaned over to whisper in his ear. She could only imagine Dylan admonishing Easton for the laugh.

"Yes, sure, fine. If that's what you really want." Toby sighed. "Anything else I should know about, Stew?"

Stewart shook his head. "Nope, that's it." He fell onto his butt and picked up a truck and a dinosaur and began crashing them together.

Voice strained, Toby said, "Bexlee."

"Yeah?"

"Are you busy Tuesday night? Have a date or anything?"

"Are you asking if I'm busy on Halloween?"

He slumped. "I'm the newest guy at the fire station. I was put on night duty all this week. I have to go in an hour from now. I can't take Stew out. I was hoping his favorite aunt could."

Bexlee laughed. "I'm technically his least favorite aunt as well. But sure, I can do it." She looked over at Jolly and Tim, Rainy's parents, who looked tired. "How about it, Mom and Dad? I could take your rugrat out, too; give you two a night off."

Both their heads popped up like prairie dogs at a loud sound.

Sitting on the floor with the kids, Joyce snickered. "I'll join you with the kids trick or treating. I love hanging out with these two. The four of us, costumes, and lots of sugar. Sounds like my kind of night."

Blake, who sat on a couch with her partner, Maria, asked, "Are you sure, Mom? You love sitting and playing with the kids, but running after them for hours on the street?"

Joyce glared at her daughter. "Are you implying I can't keep up with them?"

A wicked smile crossed the blonde's face. "Never."

Bexlee heard the door open, and Jett walked in. Jett was new to the pack. She recently started college at UC Santa Cruz. She'd actually found the person in the report Bexlee was working on. *It almost felt like my reading of this report brought her to pack house.*

As Jett rounded the corner she looked at the room full of people, then focused on Tamsin, the alpha of the pack. "Is Paige around?"

Despite who she'd asked, Maria nodded. "She's up in her suite."

Tamsin, who sat in another single recliner chair on the other side of the room, smiled warmly at Jett. Paige was Tamsin's partner and probably knew why Jett had really ventured from the campus to town. "She said she was expecting you. She'll be down soon. We've been packing up all the stuff in the bathroom to move to the guest bathroom on this floor. It's going to be a mess while construction is going on. How long did you say it'd take?"

Bexlee shook her head, finally remembering. Jett did interior design before starting college. Paige's wedding gift to Tamsin was a new bathroom area for their alpha suite.

Jett sat on the couch next to Maria. "About four weeks to get everything you wanted."

"Everything you *designed*." Tamsin corrected. "I know what I wanted, but your design blew that out of the water. What I want now is so much more."

Leaning back, Jett crossed her legs at her ankles. "We should really wait until the spring when you two are getting married. It is a wedding gift, not a Thanksgiving gift."

A snarl vibrated up through the alpha. "Watch it. You're not only in the pack, you're still in my English class!"

Jett chuckled. "Fair enough."

Maria shook her head. "I swear, all these wedding plans? I just want to elope. I'm going to steal Blake away in the middle of the night, and when you see us again, we'll be married."

Joyce snarled, "Don't you dare!"

At the same time Blake said, eyes sparkling, "I'm in!"

Chapter 2 - The One Missing Gets *All* the Work
Wynn

Most people hated Monday mornings. Wynn didn't hate them any more than any other work day. She had to get up and drive around idiots who didn't know how to drive or share the roads. Given the moronic way people whipped their metallic boxes of death around, she wondered why there weren't more accidents.

The early morning drive, before most people woke up, ensured Wynn didn't have to deal with traffic bullshit. It also meant she could find a place to park near her job. The small company where she worked, Brian Simms Mortgage Lenders, sat on a busy street. The one advantage to its location was the coffee shop next door—The Daily Grind.

She trudged in. One of the baristas behind the counter smiled. "The usual?"

Wynn nodded. "Please."

She headed over and swiped her watch to pay, then waited. A few minutes later, the barista handed her a large coffee with milk and sugar, and a sausage and egg sandwich.

Breakfast in hand, she went back to the office and opened it up. There was a small reception area and an L-shaped hallway leading to six private offices. At the end of the hallway was a conference room that fit up to twelve people, if they were all friendly.

Wynn's office was at the corner of the L. It wasn't the biggest office, but she liked having windows on two walls. She placed her bag from the coffee shop on her light-colored oak desk. The warm real wood of her desk always gave her joy.

The two monitors of her computer flared to life once she turned on her system. She placed the coffee on a coaster then slipped to the break room for a cup of the sweet tea she always stocked for herself and the friends who worked with her. It was the small things that made her happy.

She turned on her computer and began planning out her day. She didn't have clients coming in until after lunch, but there was her weekly Monday meeting with all the loan officers at nine.

She sipped her coffee and wondered if anything interesting would happen at the meeting. The answer to that was usually, 'no', but it was always a possibility.

Wynn wasn't the first to enter the conference room at nine. There were already two people there, Korah and Silas, discussing their weekend adventures.

"I went whitewater rafting with my boyfriend," Silas said, smirking at Korah and Wynn as if he knew they weren't dating anyone. "He's a model, did you know that?"

Of course, we know that, dipshit. You tell us every chance you get. Wynn sat on the other side of the table from them, trying to stay out of their conversation.

"Do you have any pictures?" Korah leaned in, eyes wide as Silas pulled out his phone.

Wynn tried not to roll her eyes. If Silas was happy, that was all that mattered.

Korah sighed. Wynn looked up and saw Korah gazing enviously at Silas's boy toy. "I stayed home with my cats."

Silas's face crumpled into one of concern. "What happened to that boyfriend of yours, Jerry?"

She shrugged. "We broke up last week. He was ... well, we just weren't working out."

That was an understatement. When Korah wasn't kissing up to Silas, she was a good person. Wynn often spent time hanging out at Korah's house. They periodically had wine and movie nights.

Jerry was a first-rate ass. He used her for her money, then slept around with other women, and men. When he did spend time with Korah, he made her feel like rubbish. Wynn was thrilled the jerk was out of her life.

Silas placed his hand on hers. "Oh sweety." He sounded so insincere. "Maybe you two will figure it out. Go to counseling, make it work."

Wynn winced as Korah nodded. "Yeah, maybe."

Wynn was about to say something when Jael came in and plopped down next to her. She forced herself not to jerk from the stench. It was times like this she hated being a werewolf even more than the monthly need to run. Having a superpower nose wasn't an asset when you were forced to sit by a colleague who bathed infrequently and smoked a lot of pot. She swore she'd get a contact high just sitting near him.

Finally, five minutes later, Brian walked in. He took the seat at the head of the table. Searching their faces, his brow creased. "Anyone know where Meghan is? Did she call in sick?"

Wynn realized she'd missed the fact that Meghan was gone, which was weird since she was one of the only other loan officers at the company she liked spending time with. She pulled out her phone, but there weren't any texts. Half-listening to what Brain said, she texted Meghan, asking her where she was.

"Since Meghan isn't here, we'll assign the job to her. I'll have Sophia send her the details."

He took notes to give to the business secretary who stayed stationed by the door during these meetings.

Wynn wasn't sure what she'd missed. With an internal kick to herself, she massaged her temples, and got back into the meeting.

Forty-five minutes later, Brian was done filling them in on a review of the previous week—clients, goals, successes and failures—and what was on the docket for this week.

Wynn gathered her stuff and headed to her office. She stopped in the staff room for some of the sweet tea she'd made and brought from home. It helped center her when her days got sour.

Once in her office, she tried to lose herself in some follow-up with clients from last week. If she could make it until lunch, then her Monday would be half over.

Chapter 3 - Trick or Treat
Bexlee

"**B**ut Bexlee, you have to wear an outfit, too!" Rainy stomped her foot and glared at Bexlee, her face screwed up in determination. "It's the rules when you go out trick-or-treating."

"It's the rules for kids, Rainy—not for the adults who chaperone."

"No." She sounded like her mom. Very bossy. "If you want to go out with us, you need a costume."

Behind Rainy, Joyce held a blank face save for a single eyebrow that rose. "What will it be, Bexlee, are you in or are you out? I'm going as a cat."

"All you have is a black jacket, jeans, and those silly ears. That's your costume?"

"It's more than you have."

Bexlee wanted to pull her hair out. This wasn't what she'd signed up for. "Fine. Give me a minute." She stomped up to her bedroom and searched her closet. When she'd been in high school she loved going to renaissance fairs. *I know I have a wench's dress somewhere in my collection of things I never throw away.* She stubbed her toe on a box labeled, 'fun stuff.'

She tore it open and found the dress. A friend had made it out of thick tapestry material. There was an olive green dress with small white, red, and pink flowers. It had white puffy sleeves. A sleeveless wine-colored corduroy top went over the dress, attaching at the waist. Once latched at the front, the top covered all but a triangle of green skirt and a bit of the bodice.

Since the skirt covered her feet, Bexlee put on a pair of sneakers, and jogged back downstairs. Stew's eyes widened. "You can be a princess with me!"

Rainy face lit up. "*Now* you can go out with us." Joyce simply smiled.

The four of them headed out with bags. The sun was beginning to set, the sky a darkening blue, with stars beginning to peak out. The buzz of voices saturated the air as the sidewalks filled with ghosts, superheroes, monsters, and mummies. Though the day had been warm, there was a light breeze, and everyone ran with their crowd, smiling at the costumes, and waving at friends. Bexlee and Joyce didn't recognize any of the other families, but that didn't bother them. They were content to take Rainy and Stew out as long as they wanted to celebrate the night.

They traversed the streets around the pack house, knocking on doors. The two kids demanded their due in candy. Some parents handed chocolate out to Bexlee and Joyce, figuring the parents needed fortification for the evening as well.

Kids ran all around. Some with parents, some in mobs ten to twenty strong. Rainy walked the sidewalk as if she owned it. Stewart stayed close to Bexlee, watching the chaos, clinging to her hand.

Bexlee glanced at his blue dress. It looked good on the boy. She'd complimented him before they left. "So, Stewart, why a princess and not a prince?"

"I don't know. Sometimes I want to be the princess, sometimes I want to be a prince. Dad always wants me to be the prince. I don't know why. Both are fun to play."

Rainy smiled at him over her shoulder. "You can borrow any of my dresses you want."

He gave her a small smile back. "Thanks. I like dresses. And jeans. Aunt Bexlee, why does it matter which one I wear? Dad says I shouldn't wear the dresses."

"I don't know why anyone thinks it matters. I'll speak with him. You can wear whatever you want. I'll make sure he knows."

His smile took over his face and he skipped ahead to catch up with Rainy.

Joyce slowed down to walk beside her. "Is that going to cause a problem between you and Toby?"

Bexlee snorted. "I've been fighting with my big brother my whole life. This issue is bigger than him. If Stewart is exploring what's comfortable, and Toby wants him to grow up happy, then he'll let the boy wear what he wants to wear."

"Well, I guess that's that."

They continued to canvas the neighborhood, collecting candy from each of the homes they visited.

Chapter 4 - Loan Officer ... Lone Wolf ... Loaning Lone Wolf
Wynn

It may still be Day of the Dead for some of her friends, but her office hadn't been dead. Wynn couldn't believe the number of people going through the Mortgage office. She'd helped two couples finalize purchasing their homes and assisted two others with figuring out their pre-approval paperwork.

She'd skipped her planned lunch out to eat a quick salad at her desk. She knew as a werewolf that wasn't enough, but her dad had called. She'd closed her door for privacy, not that anyone would listen in, but she was always cautious.

He couldn't help teasing her about being a lone loan wolf. It was one of his favorite 'dad jokes.' Afterward, he got serious. "Why didn't you tell me there was a pack in town, Wynn?"

"When I moved, they had that stupid crazy alpha. You heard about him. I didn't want anything to do with ... that."

He sighed. "But now? The new alpha has taken care of it. I still don't like knowing you're living in a city with a pack. We've always lived away from those Kool-aide drinking morons. You stay safe, and if they get too close, you run. You hear me, they don't like lone wolves, even a loan lone wolf!"

Wynn rolled her eyes. "I know, Dad. I'll be careful."

"We lived in the middle of nowhere for a reason, darlin'. There weren't any packs around. Don't be dumb."

She'd heard this her whole life. "You didn't raise me to be dumb. I have to go. I love you."

"Love you too, darlin'."

She got off the phone shortly after that for a client meeting. She had no intention of allowing any of the Pacific Pack wolves to find her. She lived her life, they lived theirs, and the city was big enough for none of them to be the wiser about her.

There was a bar close to the office she liked to go to after hard days, The Silver Fox. It was one that the local police officers frequented, but that just meant it was safe.

Wynn sat in a corner, sipping her gin and tonic. There was a couple that loved to challenge newcomers at darts. *I swear, they're racking up thousands, hustling strangers. Ah! They have their latest mark ... and they've messed up their first game. In for the kill.*

The bar had a dance floor in the center, and the scent of sweat, perfume, and cologne from the dancers wafted up, mixing with the smell of the alcohol. It was relaxing watching the dancers. Some of the couples were even decent. *Ouch! That guy just was told 'no' in the most honest way possible.*

The cops took up half the bar and a couple of tables on the other side of the room. Most in uniform, though, some wore street clothes.

It wasn't that Wynn minded being close to them, she just wanted to be in a bit of a quieter area.

The group tended to get loud, letting off steam from what seemed to be a rough day or week.

Where she sat, she could watch the motion of everyone, the dancers, the drinkers, and the flirters. At one point she thought she'd find a partner coming here, but she soon realized all the other patrons appeared to be straight, despite being in California. She only observed men approaching women, and women sizing up men.

When she first moved here, almost a year ago, she'd been so excited. All her life, living in the closet, she'd heard about the depravity of people in California. All the gays. When she had an opportunity to move across the country, away from the small town where she'd grown up, she jumped at it. Since living here, she'd only dated one woman, and it hadn't been anything like she'd hoped.

Wynn imagined finding someone to share her life with would be simple once she'd moved to Santa Cruz. This city was much the same as back home. People living their lives, day by day, trying to make ends meet. She still wasn't sure where to find her happily ever after.

She knew she should find a better bar, or maybe a dating app, or something, but she wasn't ready for all that. Too many books had her wishing the woman of her dreams would suddenly appear in her life unexpectedly. They wouldn't have to be best friends right away, but there'd be something. And then, after some tense situations, they both realize they were better off together.

Don't be a fool, Wynn. Those books always involve too much unrealistic sex and a lot of people dying. Just go to a gay bar, find a hot woman, and start living.

Despite her self-admonition, she knew she'd continue coming to The Silver Fox: they mixed great drinks, and sitting maudlin, grousing to herself about her life had become her thing.

Picking up her drink to take another sip, a new scent wafted to her. Wynn nearly choked on the gin and tonic. She slammed the glass down, coughing.

She squinted, scanning everyone around her. There were too many people to pin anything to the scent other than a direction. She searched the faces, but it wasn't like you could tell another werewolf by their look. Someone else in the bar was a wolf, and Wynn had to know who. Her pulse skyrocketed and she balled her fists to stop herself from trembling. Was it one of the pack? Another lone wolf? Would the wolf try to fight her?

Am I in danger?

Chapter 5 - Just One of The Gang
Bexlee

"**Y**ou think Halloween brings out the crazies—" Cyrus said, "—wait until you see what happens next week with the full moon." Cyrus, her partner, had been on the force for ten years. He'd had a few other partners over the years, but Bexlee couldn't figure out why they kept changing. He seemed competent and nice, though she'd only known him for a week. He tipped back his beer, finishing the last of the mug. "Every month, without fail, the moon cranks up the bizarre. Just because the sister planet in the sky is full, people can't control themselves."

Bexlee raised her mug of beer in salute. "If it's anything like my last job, next week will be a hoot."

Cyrus threw his head back and roared. "Did you just say 'hoot'? Girl, you are a trip. Where did you come from?" He waved at the bartender. "Hey, Dixie, two more beers."

"Actually, I grew up here. In Santa Cruz, that is—not the bar—but I left for school and my first job when I was eighteen. So, I've been away for almost ten years."

He just shook his head, his carrot-colored curls shaking as he laughed at her. "You're still a baby."

She yelled as she spoke to be heard over the music. "Aren't you, like, thirty-four? That's barely older than me."

He shrugged, then changed the subject. "I know you've heard about all my partners, the ones that have left, but I'm hoping to keep you. You're a real riot."

Since he'd opened up the topic, Bexlee leaned back, and narrowed her eyes at him. "Why *have* you had so many partners? You've been on the force, what, ten, eleven years. What's the deal? Should I be scared?"

He waggled his red eyebrows at her. "Probably. I eat new officers for lunch. But you don't look to have enough meat on your bones to make a good enough meal."

"Ha. Ha." She deadpanned. "Okay, fine, so you're not going to tell me. But realize—" she narrowed her eyes more, and pointed at him, "—I'm not easily gotten rid of."

"Duly noted, but I did say I was keeping you. How much have you had to drink? Should I be worried?"

Bexlee rolled her eyes.

Cyrus chuckled. "Stuck with a half-sized officer."

"I'm not half-sized. I'm five-eight. Just because you're, like, a foot taller than me, doesn't make me tiny. You're a giant."

"Only half a foot, and you seem much smaller than five-eight. Are you sure you're not deluding yourself about that height?"

She threw a handful of peanuts at him, and Cyrus laughed, as did a few cops at the next table over.

Bexlee gazed at the room full of men dancing with women. This wasn't her type of bar, but it would have to be if she wanted to get in good with the other officers. This was part of the job—social networking. She and Cyrus spoke a lot during the day, and right now it was just them at their table, but that could change at any moment. Tonight was about being out as one of the gang, and it mattered.

At her old job, she'd started with a kid who didn't like to drink, so he never went out to the bar with everyone else. He missed out on everything, including promotions. Bexlee learned her lesson from watching him.

For a moment, a scent cut through that of the dancers and beer. *Is that a werewolf? Could there be another wolf in the room?*

She quickly scanned everyone she could see, but she didn't recognize anyone. She knew there could be a non-pack wolf at the bar, but in this crowd, short of walking around sniffing, she'd never find the person. *Does Tamsin know about a lone wolf? Would she share with the rest of us?*

The scent was already gone. *Maybe I imagined it. Could I just be trying to find something interesting, a reason to move around? No one here wants to do anything but sit and drink beer or dance with the opposite sex.*

When two other officers joined the table where she and Cyrus sat, Bexlee sighed and settled in to hear a story about a harrowing arrest.

Chapter 6 - Wolf's Out of The Bag
Wynn

The blaring of Wynn's alarm pulled her from her sleep and she groaned. She'd stayed out too late drinking Thursday night, and now all she wanted to do was sleep in.

One of her favorite client couples were scheduled to come in at eleven, and she needed to get some paperwork done before they showed up. Mr. and Mrs. Wilde had bought their first house five years ago. Now that they were planning on having kids, they wanted a bigger home.

Wynn yawned and stretched, then forced herself out of bed. In the bathroom, she trudged into the shower, hoping that would help her wake up. The thought of the coffee house flitted through her mind, but then she remembered Meghan. Her friend still hadn't shown up at work. Missing a day or two was one thing, but five was too many.

Meghan lived near where the pack wolves had their behemoth of a house. Wynn avoided that area, but there was an amazing coffee house, The Zesty Bean, near her friend's place. After not getting an answer from her phone call, she decided she had to go check on Meghan.

We've never gone this long without talking. I know she's on stay-cation, but I can't believe she hasn't rubbed my nose in her relaxed activities ... or lack thereof. Just a quick how-de-do. She'll be happy to see me, tease me for over reacting. A quick laugh, and I'll be back to work.

In The Zesty Bean, she ordered her standard coffee, and got a second one for Meghan. Wynn smiled as she ordered the extra coffee. The silly woman liked a mocha cappuccino with an extra shot of espresso. The pastries looked amazing, so she ordered a box to share at the office.

Wynn pulled up to a beautiful three-story home that had been converted into single floor apartments. The joke around the office was that loan officers helped their clients get their dream homes while they themselves lived in apartments.

She knocked on Meghan's door, but there was a stillness in the air. Wynn's wolf told her the full structure was empty, but there was the scent of death in the building.

Gut tensing, Wynn tried the door, it was locked. Setting the coffees on the ground, she pulled out her lock-picking tools and got to work. When she was a teen, her dad had started training her on basic life skills. He knew she didn't want to stay living in their small town in Kentucky, so he started teaching survival skills. After years of his tutelage, she knew how to shoot a gun, hand-to-hand combat, picking a lock, tell if she were being followed, and how to disappear in a crowd.

With a click, she was in. The scent of death hit her like a punch to the face, and it took everything in her not to drop the coffees and throw up. *I'm a werewolf, damn it! Stop being a wuss.*

She put the coffee on the table by the door, along with her purse, then shut the door. Wynn didn't move from the door as she took in the living room and kitchen. Nothing looked disturbed. *What happened here? Why does this place stink?*

Wynn moved slowly. The living room was neat, the couches still had the blanket on the back. No food or wine glasses out. *Did she even watch one movie while away from work?*

In the kitchen there was a single breakfast plate and wine glass on the counter next to the sink. The box of crackers was out beside the wine. It looked like she'd be back to continue with both.

Each room looked the same as on her last visit, clean and tidy. Nothing was out of place. There hadn't been a fight or altercation that she could see.

The last room she entered was Meghan's bedroom. The scent hit her, and she dropped to her knees, belly gripped in grief. That was where she found her friend. Dead in her bed.

What the fuck happened here?

Wynn started to tremble as tears burned down her face. Like every other room she'd been in, she didn't touch anything, she'd been taught better than that, but her friend was dead.

Cheeks wet, she made her way back to her purse, she had to be responsible. In a side pocket, she found her phone and dialed the police. She wanted to run, but she'd already dialed, and the police would have her number.

It didn't take long for a couple of officers to arrive. It was early and maybe they were close? There was a solid knock on the door. Wynn opened to see two officers. A tall man with short red hair, freckles, and blue eyes. His tag read Ezra. Wynn thought she recognized him from the bar. Next to him was a petite woman with short blond hair, blue eyes, and an open friendly demeanor, despite the situation. Her tag read Court and she would've been pretty, sexy even—if she weren't a werewolf. The last thing Wynn needed right now, after finding one of her only friends dead, was to be discovered by the local pack.

For fuck's sake!

Chapter 7 - Surprising Evidence
Bexlee

A yawn blurred the report Bexlee attempted to write. She stretched and rubbed her shoulders. She'd stayed out at the bar with the gang until past midnight and then had to be at work at six-thirty this morning. Not having time to make coffee at home, she'd stopped at The Zesty

Bean, which was becoming one of her favorite stops, located near the pack house and on the way to work, and got a coffee and a cherry scone.

Next to her, Cyrus eyed the scone. "I'm not saying you had to get me one, I'm just saying we're partners. Partners do things for each other."

"Like bringing in a scone?"

"Yes!" he said with feeling. "Exactly. You went to that coffee shop, they make excellent scones, and we're both tired. It would've been ... friendly."

Bexlee took a sip of her coffee, not awake enough for Cyrus's exuberance. "I'm guessing as long as I was getting you a scone, coffee would've been nice as well?"

"I mean ... I wouldn't turn down coffee. Black, splash of milk. I mean, if you're curious."

Bexlee chuckled. "Fine, I'll keep that in mind. And if I go to The Zesty Bean again before work, what type of scone do you like?"

"Chocolate croissant."

"Noted."

The two of them got to work, finishing up their reports.

Bexlee was dotting her last 'i' when Cyrus's phone rang. She closed the folder to listen in.

His voice was curt as he answered, "Ezra." He made "UmHmm," sounds as he wrote down some notes.

Bexlee's hearing was good, but she couldn't hear what the other person said. She shut her eyes and focused. "Part of your case. The woman on the scene said no obvious cause of death."

Another possible heart attack? Don't jump to conclusions, Bex, all the person said was there was a death.

She started organizing her desk, waiting for Cyrus to tell her they were heading out. When she got done, she jotted down some notes about the current case. It was Friday and she knew she wouldn't remember much come Monday.

"Court, with me."

Bexlee snapped out of her thoughts, leaped from her seat, and grabbed her stuff in one motion. Cyrus was halfway to the door, confident she'd be behind him. She scurried to catch up, jumping into the passenger side of the car before Cyrus took off.

"Body found in an apartment. The woman who found it said her friend had been missing from work since Monday. She went to check on her today."

Bexlee scrunched up her nose. "She waited five days? Not that good of friends, then."

"Maybe, or maybe the one who was gone is known for being absent. If you want to make detective, you start by getting the facts without judgment."

Deflated, Bexlee slumped in her seat. "Fair enough. Okay, so, a dead body in an apartment. Any sign of struggle? Drugs? Alcohol?"

"Figuring that out is our job—yours really. I'll talk with the witness while you search. The person who called it in said 'no,' but she's a civilian, not a police officer. We need to figure this out ourselves."

"Got it." Bexlee agreed with Cyrus. No bystander could do the job they'd been trained for. This 'friend' may think everything appeared normal, but could've easily overlooked something.

It didn't take long to get to the apartment building, located in a nice neighborhood. When they got to the second floor apartment, Cyrus knocked. After the woman answered, Bexlee noticed her high-styled, brown curly hair, penetrating hazel eyes, red-rimmed with tears. The woman was beautiful, she was also a werewolf—a lone wolf—and she glared at Bexlee.

An oppressive feeling rose between them, as if they'd known each other for years, and had always hated each other. Bexlee shook her head. "Hi, I'm

Officer Court, this is Officer Ezra, we're here about the call you made."

Cyrus gazed back and forth between them, eyes narrowed. He may have been human, but the tension was palpable.

The lone wolf shook her luscious hair. *Is she a model? Gods above, she's someone at a crime scene, her friend just died, stop thinking this way!* "Officers, thank you for coming. My name is Wynn Taylor. The body is in the bedroom." As tight as Ms. Taylor held herself, her voice wavered with emotion.

Cyrus held out his hand and she took it, then he said, "If you'll lead the way, Ms. Taylor, my partner will just have a look around."

The two headed off, and Bexlee shivered as the strain in the air lessened. She pulled out her phone. The name 'Wynn Taylor' was familiar to Bexlee. A big name in the mortgage game, she was even in some of the commercials for a company in town. Flipping to Tamsin's contact, Bexlee texted her alpha. Hey, I'm at the scene of a crime and ran into Wynn Taylor from all those ads, you know, the obnoxious ones. Well, apparently she's a lone wolf.

She put her phone in her pocket and started doing her assigned work. The kitchen was clean, very little alcohol, and all the bottles were full. Nothing in the garbage or stashed away. After going through everything, Bexlee was confident the owner of the apartment hadn't died because of something in the kitchen.

As she moved to the bathroom, her phone vibrated. On checking the display, she saw Tamsin had replied, Thanks. I'll look into it. Don't do anything rash.

What does she think I'll do? Try to take Wynn down? Challenge her to a fight? Convert her to Wiccan? Bexlee shook her head and continued her search.

Wynn found her in the living room. "Your partner said I could go. I have things to do at work. He has my contact information. Was there anything you needed from me?"

"Besides the obvious?"

The other woman sighed. "Yeah, besides that. Any chance it'll stay between us?"

"Too late for that, but it wouldn't happen anyway. It's not a safe option, especially with everything going on. I can't talk much now ... you understand." It wasn't a question.

Wynn darted a look towards the room where Cyrus was. "Here's my card." She handed Bexlee a card with her name, number, and several social media contacts. "If you're willing, I'd like to talk with you and give you my side."

Bexlee sighed. "Sure, Ms. Taylor, I'll give you a call later."

"Please, call me Wynn." Despite the peasantry of the conversation, Wynn still held herself tightly as she turned towards the door.

Bexlee grunted and watched her leave; she was as nice to watch leave as she was to see coming. *Gah! Stop it Bex! She's a lone wolf and probably dangerous!*

Cyrus strutted out from the room. "Did you just get a date at a crime scene? Damn, Court, respect!"

Chapter 8 - Rules of The Game
Tamsin

"**D**o you have to do this alone?" Paige sat on the edge of the bed watching Tamsin dress. Her eyes followed her partner's every move. If Paige didn't watch out, Tamsin would pounce, and her morning would start much later. It was Saturday; she had time.

"I don't, but since she's a lone wolf who's been avoiding us, I don't want to show up with the entire pack. I figured one-on-one will be less intimidating."

Paige sighed. "I guess. But are there any laws against what she's doing? Like, is there a punishment system?"

"No laws, it's convention, a politeness. There's the way things are done."

"So, what are you hoping to accomplish by confronting her?" Paige rubbed her temples. "I want to understand all the ways of the wolves. Why can't it just be easy?"

Tamsin walked over to Paige, straddled her, and kissed her. With a groan, she backed away, knowing she really didn't have time to play with her mate.

She'd had Bexlee find Wynn's home address. It wasn't exactly within her job description, but since Bexlee had it, Tamsin didn't feel too guilty asking for it. The house was on the other side of town—as if Wynn had tried to stay clear of the pack. The more Tamsin contemplated it, the more she thought that was exactly it.

She parked in front of the small yellow ranch-style house with a cobblestone walkway up to the door. Tamsin rang the doorbell and waited. It didn't take long for a woman, a bit shorter than her with brown curly hair and hazel eyes, to open the door. The sneer and glare told Tamsin exactly how happy she was to see her.

"What are you doing here?"

"We need to talk."

"No, we don't." Wynn started to shut the door, but Tamsin put her hand out to stop it.

"Look, Wynn, you won't be able to keep me out. We may as well talk civilly." Tamsin stood in the doorway, her hand braced, eyeing the other wolf.

With a snarl, she whipped around. "Fine. But once we're done I don't want to see or hear from you or any of your pack. You *are* the alpha, right?"

Tamsin snorted. "We'll see." She responded to the first comment, though she realized Wynn may think she answered the second.

She was led through a tidy living room into a kitchen with a small table. "Have a seat. Coffee, tea, soda, water?"

"Whatever is most convenient."

Wynn scrunched up her face, looking annoyed. "I just brewed a pot of coffee. How do you take it?"

"Milk or cream, if you have it."

Once they each had a mug of coffee, Wynn sat opposite her. "What do you want ... wait, did you give me your name?"

Fuck, I am too much in my head. Just because I know her, doesn't mean I know her. I need to get better at this, get a routine. Except a routine means we have more lone wolves, and I don't want that.

Tamsin held out her hand. "Hi, I'm Tamsin, alpha of the Pacific Pack here in Santa Cruz."

Wynn shook Tamsin's hand quickly, then wiped her hand on her jeans. "So, Tamsin, what are you doing here?"

"Before you moved to Santa Cruz, did you live in an area with a pack? Were you ever part of a pack?"

With a sigh, the other woman sipped her coffee. "No and no."

"It is standard to talk with a pack if you want to live in a pack city as a lone wolf."

"And, alpha, have *you* ever lived as a lone wolf?" There was a bite to her words.

"Actually, yes. For five years I lived in Chicago. When I moved there, I checked in with the alpha. He gave me places in the city where I could live and run so I wouldn't bump into his pack."

"Well, you don't have to do that, do you? I've lived here for almost a year, and you never even knew. If my being a lone wolf in your territory was going to be an issue, I'd think it would've come up early on in your reign as alpha, what, a few months ago, don't you?"

Tamsin clenched her jaw for a moment, not wanting to snap. *She did know who I was. Probably knew my name when I came into the house, too.* With a skill born of working with teens for years, Tamsin smiled pleasantly. "Probably. But I took over as alpha in late May and started a new job in August. It's been just over five months, and I've been pretty busy with the new wolves, new job, and new city. Under the circumstances, I don't believe me not realizing you were around shows ill on me. I've been building a welcoming community. In reality, since you seem to know there was a change in alpha, *you* should've taken the initiative, and I think you know that. Moreover," Tamsin took a breath to calm her heart that started beating faster, "Not that it's much of your business, but my pack had been decimated. It was down to four wolves. I am slowly building it up. Being a lone wolf in Santa Cruz without us knowing *will* be an issue."

"But not for me." Wynn raised an eyebrow. "You know about me now, so we're past all that." She waved her hand. "So, I'll continue staying out of all your wolves' way, running outside of the city limits, and everything will be hunky-dory."

"Is there a reason you don't want to interact with other wolves?" Tamsin cocked her head, interested.

"I just don't. It's my business, alpha." Wynn bristled. Her eyes narrowed and her voice deepened.

Tamsin rubbed her face. "I guess it is. I would like you to come to pack house and meet the other wolves. That—"

"Why?" Wynn snapped. "What possible reason would I have to put myself through all that?"

"Well, if you'd let me finish. That way, if any of them run into you, they'll know who you are, and that you've already spoken to me. No more surprises."

Tamsin saw Wynn clench her jaw and ball her fists. She was holding in some real anger. "I'll pass. You can just tell them about me, or have that Bexlee chick do it."

Maintaining her calm demeanor, Tamsin continued. "Fine. No meeting the other wolves. If any of them decide to buy a house, I'll tell them to avoid Brian Simms Mortgage. I'll tell the witches as well. It will save on questions."

"I don't think all that is necessary. No reason to take work away from my colleagues. But if you feel you must, I won't stop you."

Tamsin took another slow breath, trying to calm her frayed nerves. This woman could get under her normally calm demeanor. Students couldn't do it this well. "I will see you around, Wynn Taylor."

Wynn's brows rose as she gave a tight fake smile. "I certainly hope not, Tamsin, alpha of the Pacific Pack."

Chapter 9 - Nobody Likes a Monday
Bexlee

The Zesty Bean opened at four in the morning. That was part of its magic. Bexlee had to be at work by six on Monday morning, so she planned on stopping in early for breakfast and coffee. At five-fifteen she walked in, ordered coffee and an egg and sausage sandwich and sat at a table with her phone. She wanted a few quiet minutes to wake up before she started her day.

At just after five-thirty she ordered two more coffees and two chocolate croissants. Halfway to the door, her phone rang.

"Bexlee here." She stifled a yawn.

"Bex, it's Cyrus. We're being called to a scene, where are you?"

Her heart started to pound. "At The Zesty Bean."

"Tell me you have coffee for me."

"I do, and chocolate."

"You're my favorite of all my partners." His voice purred over the phone. "I figure from that date you arranged that you don't swing my way, so I can flirt all I want."

Bexlee chuckled. "I don't know, you're awfully cute with your red hair and freckles. Don't leave a girl hanging."

Cyrus snorted. "I see you through the door, hop in the car."

Bexlee pocketed her phone before hurrying out and getting in the car. She handed Cyrus a coffee. "What happened?"

"A car crash. We're the closest car." He put on the siren, and they were off.

It didn't take them long to get to the site. Cyrus pushed through the rubber neckers and pedestrian gawkers to the police line, well past the broken glass and car detritus littering the ground. A couple of officers in uniform were redirecting traffic around the mess.

There were two cars, both mangled. Bexlee narrowed her eyes. "A blue Toyota Camry with California plates hit a red Ford Focus with Oregon plates."

Cyrus parked and they both got out and put on gloves. Bexlee approached the Camry. Inside were a man and a woman. She could hear the ambulance approaching. The window was open. "Hello? Are either of you okay?"

There was no response.

She reached in and felt the neck of the driver. Her head was bleeding from where it had struck the steering wheel. She couldn't find a pulse. Moving to the passenger side, she could see where a piece of glass had impaled itself into the man's face. Swallowing against the gore, she reached in to find a pulse, and unsurprisingly found nothing.

She stepped back, shaking her head. "Nothing here. Both dead on arrival."

Cyrus's gaze snapped to her from the Ford Focus. "The driver here is alive, help me release the seat belt. Can you get in over there?"

As she moved where he indicated she heard the siren of more emergency vehicles approaching.

She climbed in the passenger back seat and scooted to the center. With a tug, she got the belt released. She had to use werewolf strength; nothing even her partner could've done. Once the woman was free of the belt, they maneuvered her from the car. The ambulance arrived, and they got her onto a stretcher and the EMTs took it from there.

She and Cyrus moved back to the Toyota. "Can you tell what caused the accident?"

Shutting her eyes, Bexlee took in a slow, long breath of air. "I don't smell anything, alcohol, pot, drugs. We'll need the medical assistant to do a full autopsy, but my gut is telling me we can rule out any substance."

Cyrus reached in and looked at the woman's arms. "There aren't any needle marks, which lends to your conclusion. She also isn't wearing a med alert bracelet. If she has epilepsy or some other condition, it isn't bad enough to warn others."

"I wonder what caused it." Bexlee gazed at the dead faces of the two young people.

"We'll know in a few days. It could be another mysterious heart attack. I swear, they are all connected, I just don't know how." Cyrus wrapped his hands behind his neck. "How can heart attacks be contagious?"

It took a few more hours to process the scene. They'd collected the personal information, along with individual effects, and waited for the tow truck to take away the vehicles.

By the time they could leave, Bexlee was thrilled she'd had a second cup of coffee. When she and Cyrus returned to the station or arrived, it was almost time for lunch.

Chapter 10 - One is The Loneliest Number
Wynn

As Wynn drove from the city, heading south, she wanted to scream. Her meeting with Mr. and Mrs. Wilde had been canceled, not because of her, but because they hadn't shown up. She didn't usually get ghosted by her clients, and it frustrated her when it happened. She'd called and left messages for them, but so far she hadn't heard back.

Have they decided to stay in their current home? Is it a matter of money? Did they find a different loan officer? Was it something I did? I wouldn't be upset if they changed their mind on moving ... just tell me! Cancel the meeting. I've never been cross with them!

Wynn had been asking herself these questions all day.

In a fit of aggravation, she hit the *hands free connect* on the car's steering wheel. "Call Dad."

The phone rang once. "Hey darlin', why're you calling me now?" His honied tone seeped through the line. "You know I'm about to go out for a run."

"I know; I'm driving to a safe place to run myself, I just ... the pack found me."

"Are you safe? Are they going to eliminate you?" He sounded pissed.

"No Dad, it isn't like that. The alpha invited me to dinner so the other pack members would know me. That way I could be in the city and the others wouldn't be surprised if they saw me."

"Don't trust that ass, he's just trying to trick you so it's easier to clean up." Code for kill. Her dad had never been one for subtlety.

"First off, sexist much? The alpha's a woman. And second, I can smell a lie as easily as you can. She wasn't trying to deceive me. She'd been a lone wolf for a while in Chicago."

"Look, Wynfrey, I raised you to be smarter than this. Pack wolves are brutes. They come in, clear out the good old family wolves, and take over a place. I can't force you to move, but darlin', you need to think about looking for a new job far away from those killers."

Wynn wanted to scream, then tear the steering wheel from the car and wallop her dad with it. He wasn't listening to her. "I'll be safe, I promise."

She hung up and focused on driving. It didn't take long before she arrived in Monterey. She parked, stripped, stored her clothes in the car, and began shifting to her wolf. The shift took several minutes. If she shifted more regularly, then her wolf would flow over her like water, but since she waited for the moon, it was slower. Her bones shortened and snapped, reforming to the animal shape. Hair retreated and regrew. Her fingers shortened to paws and then she stood on four feet ... paws.

With a howl, she was ready to run and worship the moon's beauty. The large orb in the sky pulled on her soul, its magic feeding her need to run with whiskers and a tail. She often tried to ignore her wolf side, but for one night a month she had an overwhelming need to shift. Once a wolf, Wynn felt alive in a way she rarely did living alone as a human.

The small area she selected had grass and a few trees, and, as luck would have it, a small rabbit trail. Slinking in low and quiet, she found a plump beast, snatched it up, and ate. Then she was off. No more hunting, just time for a run and play. She didn't give over to this side of herself much, but she'd let the wolf rule for the rest of the night.

When she was out running, she could release all the tension and control she put on herself as a human. All the pressure melted away with the here-and-now attitude of the wolf.

Her wolf wasn't scared of the pack; she wanted to meet other wolves, run with them, and have contact. Part of Wynn wondered if the reason she was so snappish was because she denied herself human interaction. She knew when she lived with her dad she received a lot of small touches, and it seemed to feed a need. Now that she lived in a city alone and by herself, she was going a bit bonkers.

Wynn stopped running as the full realization of what she just thought hit her. *I wonder if that Bexlee*

*woman will call me. I don't want to join the pack,
but having a no strings attached romping partner
would dampen*
     I wonder if she'd agree ...

Chapter 11 - This is *Not* a Date
Bexlee

The piles of paperwork Bexlee had to sort through made her head swim. If she did nothing but cross her Ts and dot her Is, then it would take her until the weekend to finish it all. With a sigh, she took a sip of coffee and dug into the piles.

An hour later her work load didn't look any different, though her head was feeling worse. It wasn't that she hated doing paperwork, it wasn't her favorite, but she knew the value of organization. The problem was, most of the files she sorted through were from before her time. Putting the final touches on her own cases was one thing, but on some other officers'—just because they were lazy and unwilling to do it themselves ... she wanted to scream.

One of the other officers did a fly-by, dropping another folder on her desk. About to snarl, she saw the names on the tab: Mr. and Mrs. Wilde.

It's the people from the car crash Monday! Now this report I'm interested in.

Bexlee pushed aside the files she'd been summarizing, and opened the one for the Wilde's. As she read, her heart dropped into her gut. "Hey, Cyrus. Did you get a copy of this file, too?"

His head snapped up from behind his own mountain on his desk. "Which one? I have so many. This Organization Thursday bullshit is just that. Whose idea was it, anyway?"

"Yours! And I'm doing your work, so stop complaining!"

"Right, fuck. Okay, yeah, the Wilde's. What about them?"

Bexlee grumbled. "Cy, read the thing. It'll take you a minute—unless all the paperwork has left you addled."

"I tell you, Bex, it may have, it just may have. Okay, give me a sec."

As Cyrus read, so did Bexlee. She wanted to absorb more of the medical report than she had during her first glance. When she finished that, she moved on to what the forensic experts found in the car. Before she got very far, Cyrus started to swear.

"They're linked. How the fuck is this happening?" He stood and started to pace. "I mean, talking about magic and all the voodoo shit sounds insane, but we are amassing a pile of people—young healthy people—who are having deadly heart attacks, seemingly out of the blue. God damn it!" He stopped by Bexlee's desk and threw his hands out to the side in frustration. "Okay, I'll look into the family, you check out their life here: jobs, friends, family, the works. The woman was driving, she had the heart attack. The man was just a victim of circumstance. Death by car crash. It's all sorts of fucked up."

"You're losing your touch Cy, barely any swear words that time." Bexlee teased.

"Just get to work."

By eleven in the morning, Bexlee was on her fifth large mug of coffee. She thought she could hear in colors. She also knew the couple had been thinking about buying a new house. If her records were correct, their realtor told her they'd been working with Wynn as a loan officer. That's two people around Wynn who ended up dead.

Is she like Blake? Is she a witch as well as a werewolf? I didn't smell witch on her ... but maybe?

Before she could follow up on the thought, a second new report—about the ten billionth on her desk this week—was tossed on a pile by another helpful officer. She wanted to bite her, and not in a sexy, fun way.

Bexlee snatched the new folder and opened it up. Meghan Lee, age thirty-two, single, died of a heart attack. "Argh!" She bellowed.

The officer who'd tossed the file on her desk chuckled. Cyrus gazed at her, one eyebrow lifted. "Something the matter?"

"That woman, who was dead in her apartment."

"The one whose friend flirted with you?"

Bexlee couldn't control her cheeks burning. "Yeah, no, maybe, whatever. That one. I just got her report."

"Heart attack?"

She slumped. "Heart attack." Cyrus continued to stare. "I'm going to call the friend, bring her in for questioning."

"Speaking as your friend, you know she didn't do it. Why don't you just offer to meet her somewhere less intense? Let her know what happened to her friend. It doesn't have to be here. As your partner, I agree, call in our prime suspect."

Bexlee's jaw dropped. "Are you kidding me? Are you suggesting I meet up with this woman?"

"Well, it is close to lunch time." He winked.

"I am not going out on a date with a potential suspect." She hissed, narrowing her eyes at him as if he'd lost his mind.

"Bex, do you think she did it?" He didn't wait for an answer. "Now call her. She was into you. You seemed into her. You'd make a hot couple."

She squeezed her eyes shut and her fists tightly closed. Her nails bit into her palms. "Fine, I'll call her, but it is *not* a date."

Cyrus chucked as Bexlee looked for the card she'd gotten from the prickly, but sexy woman, almost a week ago.

"Wynn Taylor, how can I help you?" Wynn answered with a low smooth voice that dug its way through Bexlee's body. *Gods above, even her voice is sexy!*

"Um, hi, Ms. Taylor. It's Officer Court. We met last week. I have some information about your friend's death. We could talk here at the precinct, or if you'd like to speak somewhere else, I have a bit of time."

Bexlee heard what sounded like papers shuffling and some tapping on a keyboard. "Officer Court, you were at Meghan's house." More tapping of keys. *Is she looking me up? Am I that forgettable? Why does that thought irk me?* "Hmmm. I haven't had lunch yet. Would you be up to meeting me at Sassy Sashimi? I love their rolls."

Biting back a sigh, Bexlee agreed to meet Wynn in half an hour. Once off the phone, she glared at Cyrus. "This is *not* a date!"

She walked out to the chorus of her colleagues' laughter. Most didn't know why they were laughing. Any excuse was good enough for them.

Bexlee arrived at the restaurant first and got a table. She perused the menu. The unmistakable scent of wolf wrapped around her, followed by

Wynn's. She hadn't realized in her short meeting at the apartment, she'd gotten such a strong scent memory of Wynn. She heard her footsteps before the waitress sat her across from Bexlee.

After making her decision on what she wanted to eat, Bexlee looked up from the menu. She was again taken by the other woman's beauty. Her hazel eyes almost glowed and her brown waves shone in the soft sunlight streaming in through the windows. Bexlee swallowed by the complement that flew to her lips ... *this is not a date!*

Gods above, Bex, get ahold of yourself. What am I thinking?

Before she could say anything, Wynn asked, "Do you mind if we order before we get down to business?"

"That's fine. I've figured out my rolls. It's nice eating with someone who won't be shocked by my appetite."

Wynn smiled, and her face lit up. "I know what you mean."

Once the waitress arrived, they ordered, then Bexlee leaned back. "How much do you know about our world?"

"The furry side?"

"The magic side."

Wynn's eyes widened for a moment. "Not a lot. Where I come from, wolves are it. Anything else is kind of thought of as make-believe."

Bexlee nodded. "I wondered." Bexlee sipped a tea the waitress brought. "Your friend died of a heart attack."

Wynn's head tilted and her body tightened. Bexlee could tell she tried to hide her emotions. "Really? She was healthy. And as far as I know, both her parents are alive. Isn't that odd? She was only, what, thirty? Thirty-one? We didn't talk age much."

"Thirty-two, but yeah, to me it's odd. I'm not an expert on medical conditions, or your friend, but I think it's odd."

Wynn took a sip from the mug in front of her. "Why? Was there something off? Did I miss something when I did my visual search? I'm usually pretty good with those."

"No, nothing missed in the apartment. What you missed was the number of other people who've died of a similar cause." Her eyes got wide, and Bexlee saw her hand begin to shake. "An epidemic? A heart attack epidemic?"

"Sort of—"

Wynn's eyes widened, her facade breaking. "Wait! You asked about magic. Do you think this is something on our side? Like ... the witches? Do you think they targeted Meghan? Wait. Why would they? She was just human." Wynn spoke faster with each question, her voice getting more intense.

Bexlee waited, letting Wynn think it out. The waitress brought their food. The sushi was fantastic. They both ate while Wynn gazed at Bexlee with narrowed eyes. It was dangerously close to a glare.

"Do you think this is something I brought to my friend?" She snapped out. "Is that why you asked about witches? Do you think I had something against Meghan and asked a witch to take her out?"

Bexlee pressed her palms together and rested her chin on her thumbs. There was a fine line between sharing and giving too much information. "I'm trying to figure out how a young woman died in her apartment. My partner and I are collecting information. Right now, that is it. For all we know, Meghan died of natural causes."

Wynn relaxed. "Okay, yeah, I guess. Thank you for telling me the truth; that's something. You could've just told me about the heart attack and left it there. I guess I should be happy that you gave me anything more."

Bexlee smiled. "It isn't like I can bring this up with just anyone." She went back to eating. The food was really good.

"That's true. Your partner would probably think you were insane. Drop you like a hot potato."

Did she just call me hot? No, wait, that's a saying ... damn, stay focused.

"Maybe. He's had a few partners. I may be safe ... maybe." A smiled bubbled up on her face.

"That's good. Unless the reason he's had so many partners is he's an ass. Do you want to switch?"

"No, he seems like a great guy. I'm not sure why the others left."

Wynn took another bite of sushi. "Are you new to the area?"

"No, I grew up here, with the pack, but moved for school. You're new."

She shrugged. "Yeah. I wanted to find a bigger city. I moved here, then learned about the pack." Her lip twitched up into a sneer when she said *pack*.

"You're pretty anti-pack. I'm surprised you're sitting here with me." The full time Bexlee had been away from her pack she'd yearned to get back. She couldn't understand Wynn's aversion to being around others who understood her peculiarities and needs.

Wynn looked down at her plate, a blush coloring her cheeks. "I grew up with my dad and cousins in a small community in Kentucky. It wasn't until I snapped at your alpha that it occurred to me that maybe I needed some time with other ... or another wolf."

A chill went down Bexlee's back. "Are you asking to join the pack?"

"Gods, no. "She shivered. "Sorry." She lifted her hands up towards Bexlee, palms up. "No offense. I didn't mean it like that. I just ... no. No thank you. I don't want to join the cult." She grimaced. "I just ... I was wondering, hoping, maybe you'd like to spend some time with me."

Bexlee locked her jaw to stop her mouth from dropping open. After her head caught up, she asked, "Are you asking to date me?" *This is not a date!*

"No, well, not really. I just thought we could be ... wolves with benefits."

Chapter 12 - Wine O'clock
Wynn

Korah's wine selection was extensive. Wynn looked through the labels and found a port. They had a spread of cheese, meats, nuts, and sweets. More food than two people could eat, but they didn't want to limit themselves while they watched reality TV and gossiped.

Two glasses poured, Wynn joined her friend in the living room. They sat and sipped their port and ate some from the charcuterie board. Finally, Korah said, "That memorial service for Meghan today was really nice. Her parents did a really nice job putting it all together."

Sadness returned to Wynn. Meghan's parents were in good health and her brother had spoken about how he'd always looked up to his big sis. The two of them had been friends growing up. No one expected any health problems from the seemingly healthy woman.

"The company sent a nice bouquet of flowers," Wynn added.

"They did. Though, I'm kind of glad we were the only two to show up. It's enough to have to hang out with everyone all week. I'm surprised Silas didn't show up with his latest boy-toy."

Wynn snorted. "They're probably off somewhere being fabulous."

"True." Korah agreed. "He sure knows how to find them pretty." Korah's face fell. "Jerry wasn't pretty—or nice. I can't seem to find one who's either, let alone both."

Wynn scooted over and wrapped an arm around her friend. "Jerry's an ass. He seemed nice at first; he kept buying you flowers and boxes of chocolates. Who knew he'd turn out to be so controlling?"

"Yeah, when he started getting jealous of our wine nights, I knew things were getting to be too much."

"Is he still calling or stopping by?" Wynn tried to ask the question casually, but part of her wanted to call her cousins in and take care of the cad the old fashion way. If anyone deserved the old heave-ho, it was this jerk.

"Mostly. He's left me a few messages, but I haven't seen him in a week."

"A week?" Wynn's eyebrow shot up. "You do know you've been broken up longer than that."

"Yes, but seven days *is* a new record."

"When you start dating again, the guy is going to be confused, thinking you're still with the turd. You need to text him to leave you alone, then block the number."

"What if he shows up at the office? Or at a client's house? He knows some of my former clients."

Wynn's head started to throb. "Then you call the cops. I know one—the one who helped with Meghan. She's good. We could call her, let her know Jerry is harassing you."

"You know a cop?" She waggled her eyebrows and gave Wynn a saucy smile. "Why, Wynn, this is a whole new side of you."

"Korah, we are not changing the subject." Wynn glared, but didn't think it went well with a glass of wine in her hand and a cracker salami sandwich in the other.

"My god, you're blushing. I've never seen you blush!" Korah's mouth dropped open. "Do you like this woman? What is she like? Is she pretty? Did I know you liked women? Do you also like men? Whoa! This port is making me rambly!" She giggled.

"No dear, you are always rambly. It has nothing to do with the wine." Wynn slumped, feeling defeated by the weight of all the questions. "I think you did know I liked women, but you may have forgotten. That conversation may have happened on tequila night. You probably forgot a lot about that night. That's when you finally decided to dump Jerry the Dickwad."

"Mmm, that night was yummy. The next morning sucked, though. We discussed you that night?" Korah rubbed her eyes. "Are you sure?"

"Do you actually remember anything about that night?"

Korah narrowed her eyes, gazing at the TV. "Uh, I decided to leave Jerry because he told me I couldn't buy a purse I really wanted, even though I was using my own money. He said it was financially frivolous."

"Yep, and you'd wanted the purse for months, and it was on sale. He yelled at you, then knocked you down. It was too much."

Korah growled. It would've made Wynn's dad proud. "Why didn't *he* die of a fucking heart attack? If anyone deserves it, he does. Did you know, his ex called me a few weeks ago. She said she heard we'd broken up. Then she launched into why *they'd* broken up."

Wynn's headache was getting worse. "Why didn't she call you sooner?"

"She was afraid of him."

"For fuck's sake."

Korah lifted her glass in cheer. "Exactly!"

Chapter 13 - Choices
Bexlee

"How do I look, Dad? Do I look tough?"

Bexlee shut her book and put it on the table next to the chair she sat on. Stewart stood in front of her brother wearing a hunter green dress, combat boots, and a plastic army hat.

Toby's eyes widened and he smiled at his son. Then he darted a desperate look to Bexlee. She bit back a laugh.

She unfolded her legs, placing her feet on the floor, then leaned forward. "You look amazing, Stew. Are you planning on hiding in the woods and protecting us?"

He spun to face her with a big smile. "You figured it out! This green looks like leaves, right?"

"It sure does, hon. Where's Rainy? Has she seen you in this outfit?"

He smiled and scampered off.

Toby slumped. "Why is this so hard for me?"

"That's an excellent question. Why *is* it so hard for you? Stew is just figuring himself out."

"Are you sure?"

"I am."

"So, he'll become my son again one day?"

"For fuck's sake, Toby, he *is* your son or child, no matter what. If he decides he is a girl or nonbinary, are you going to love him any less?"

Toby's brows furrowed. "No, I'll always love him. He's my kid."

"Okay, so, what are you asking me, bro?"

He gazed off in the direction Stewart ran. "I don't know. You always encourage him. Is that what

I should be doing? Encouraging him? Should I take him out shopping? What should I do?"

"It isn't that I'm encouraging him; I'm supporting him. I'm letting him know that I love him and think he's wonderful no matter what. As for shopping, ask him. Let him define what he wants, just like any other kid. Why is it so hard for you?"

"I don't know. His mom thinks he's weird because of me ... us ... our family."

"Yeah, well, she's a bitch. You know that. It's why she's no longer around. She decided to leave the most amazing boy for idiotic reasons. Now we all get to raise him."

Toby smiled as Tamsin sauntered in with a fresh mug of coffee and sat on the loveseat. "I miss my bathroom. It had a jacuzzi tub. Showering feels like I've become a peasant."

Bexlee threw a pillow at her. "Too bad! I demand jetted tubs in all the bathrooms!"

Tamsin laughed. "Not a bad idea, really. It's a luxury, but nice. Maybe a hot tub out back would work."

Bexlee moaned. "Yeah, I'd go for that."

Paige came in and sat next to Tamsin. "Are we going out tonight? Just you and me and Thai food?"

"Not unless you've found someone else to watch the kids. I agreed to watch them both."

Paige hugged Tamsin's arm. "There's a full pack, and everyone else is busy?"

"Apparently. The only person I didn't ask was Bexlee."

The others in the room gazed at her, and she blushed.

Jaw dropping, Paige leaned forward. "Talk, woman!"

"I may have a thing."

"How did I not know this? The gossip around here is legit." Paige's eyes danced in challenge.

"Well, I'm a cop. Keeping secrets is something I usually do well. I just figured I wouldn't tell anyone." Bexlee smiled self-mockingly as her plan came to its end.

"I mean," Paige said, as she leaned back into Tamsin's half embrace, "it isn't like we're going to know the person, right? So, why all the secrecy?"

"True," Bexlee said. Werewolves could smell lies. She had to be very careful what she said. "I think I'll go get ready."

Tamsin snickered. "Bexlee, do we know the person?"

Damn, it all to hell and back! If Paige asked I could confidently have said 'no.' "This person isn't someone known to most of the pack, no. Why?"

Tamsin's brow rose. "So, I do know them. And you're keeping it on the down-low. Make sure it doesn't become an issue."

"Sounds good." Bexlee said vaguely. Her gut knotted as she scooted up to her room to change.

Wynn always looked glamorous. She decided to wear a lavender sleeveless cocktail dress that hugged her to her waist. It was simple, but brought out the blue of her eyes. *I know this isn't a date, but may as well look the part of the eventual 'benefits', right?*

Chapter 14 - Dinner of Convenience
Wynn

hy am I nervous? I'm the one who wanted to do this. It isn't like it's my first date. Wynn slipped out of her car and smoothed out the black underlayer of her dress. She wore a skin tight underdress that ended scandalously high, barely decent. It had a top with a flowing multi-layered sky blue tank-style bodice that ended at her waist. The spaghetti straps were hidden by her curly waves of hair.

She entered the Italian restaurant they'd agreed on, and found Bexlee at the hostess stand. Wynn had only seen the other woman in her police blues. Today she wore a light purple dress that kissed her curves. The material shimmered in the lights and Wynn wanted to rub her hands up Bexlee's hips and around her small waist and feel how fit the woman really was. *I bet her ass is as tight as her chest is full.*

In contrast to Wynn's tight dress, Bexlee's looked like it would flare out if she spun. It was the type of dress that would move with the wearer on the dance floor.

Dancing would be fun ... no! This is not a date. It's a means to an end. Scratching an itch. Giving my wolf some touchy-feely so she'll calm down.

Moving up to stand next to Bexlee, Wynn slid her hand into the other woman's. Bexlee clasped her hand back. *She must have smelled me when I entered.*

"Right this way," the hostess said, grabbing two menus and leading them into a maze of tables and people.

They were seated at a booth. Wynn sat across from Bexlee. They each took their menu after ordering a glass of red wine.

Wynn mumbled to herself as she looked over the selections. "This is not a date." She spent so much time with humans, she forgot that Bexlee would be able to hear her.

"So, you're saying I should order the garlic shrimp as an appetizer?"

Lowering her menu, Wynn smiled. "If that's what you want. I'd prefer the artichoke dip; it has plenty of garlic in it. We could share, then we'd both be contaminated."

Bexlee smiled wide, and Wynn had to catch her breath. The woman had a beauty she probably didn't even know about. Her short wild blond hair and sparkling blue eyes were captivating. This non-date would work just fine, as long as they could keep it light.

"Sounds good to me, but I have an older brother, so I don't share well. If I eat more than my half, you've been warned."

Wynn laughed. "I grew up with male cousins. If I can't take care of myself, then shame on me."

By the time the waitress came back, they were ready to order. They kept most of their conversation light and on their jobs.

"Your partner, Officer Ezra, he's a big guy. And not to say you can't hold your own—I can guess at how strong you are—but do you worry about being shorter than most of the others?"

Bexlee took a bite of her chicken parmesan, taking a moment to savor it. "Not really. I can kick anyone in the head."

Wynn's brow rose in appreciation of the woman's abilities.

"I just may need to kick them in the knee first to drop them."

Wynn laughed. She covered her mouth when she realized how loud she was being. Throughout the meal the two of them were having good conversation. It was more than she could've hoped for.

When the bill came, they split it, then Wynn gave Bexlee directions to her home. The alpha had found her house, and she assumed the directions had come from the police office, but she decided to play it straight, so to speak.

They separated to their own vehicles and took the quick drive to her place. The doubts she'd felt walking into the restaurant were all gone. Wynn was excited for what was coming next.

Once Bexlee parked, Wynn took her hand and led her through her house to her bedroom. She pushed the other woman against the wall and swept in for a demanding kiss. Bexlee matched her. She slid her hands into Wynn's hair and moaned as the kiss deepened.

Wynn's hands slid down Bexlee's body. She appreciated how form fitting the top of her dress was as her thumbs slid over tight nipples. With a quick intake of breath, Bexlee arched into Wynn's hands. Wynn rubbed soft circles over Bexlee's breasts, pulling back as the other woman tried to push towards her to increase the pressure.

Finally, Bexlee broke the kiss with a groan. "You're killing me."

"Good. Your dress is in my way. I'll give you what you want if you give me what I want."

"You're awfully demanding."

Wynn just looked at her with a raised brow.

Bexlee reached down, grabbing the hem of her dress, then yanked up. The dress was off in a wink. Underneath, she only wore the tiniest of undies. Wynn growled her approval. She reached out for Bexlee's hips and guided her to the bed. A slight shove, and Bexlee plopped down. It didn't take long for Wynn to divest herself of her clothes, and then she crawled up over the other woman, who scooted up to the center of the queen size bed.

When Wynn perched over Bexlee, she wanted to purr. "I need this contact. This is all about me, police wolf-woman. I'm going to have my way with you. Then, once I've had my fill, we can discuss if anything more will happen."

Bexlee squeezed her eyes shut. "So, you're just going to use me. I don't get to do anything back? No touching, licking, kissing, feeling. I just lie here?" She wasn't sure if she was excited or disappointed at the prospect.

"Would it help if I tied you down?"

A small sound of pleasure escaped the other woman as her arm covered her eyes. Her breathing got a bit ragged for a moment. "Maybe next time." She finally whispered. "For now, I'll try to behave by your rules, but gods above, that's a tall order."

Wynn smirked, then bent down to nibble on Bexlee's ear.

Chapter 15 - A Secret Amongst Friends
Bexlee

B exlee fisted the comforter to stop herself from touching Wynn. *Why did I agree to this?* Her eyes rolled back in her head as the beautiful woman trailed kisses to her chest. Her hot mouth sucked one breast in, her tongue flicking the nipple she'd played with earlier, ensuring its sensitivity.

Firey sensation flowed to her center, and her panties grew more and more wet. She arched up with a small whimper. Wynn scraped her teeth over the sensitive skin, biting down at the end. Bexlee cried out. A bit in pleasure, a bit in pain. *Gods above, Wynn is going to be my death, both literal and figurative.*

Wynn sucked in Bexlee's oversensitive breast, her other hand flicking and pinching the other. Finally, the other woman pulled away, sucking hard as she did. Chills played up and down Bexlee's body.

"Let's see what we have." Wynn's warm hand slid in Bexlee's undies. "Hmm, nice and wet. It seems you are enjoying yourself, Officer Courts." Her hand cupped Bexlee's sex right before she slid two fingers in for a couple of quick thrusts.

A small yelp of pleasure escaped Bexlee. Wynn hummed in appreciation. "Yes, very wet. But, Bexlee, your hands keep jumping up as if to join in. I just might have to tie you down next time."

Bexlee's body tightened in anticipation.

"Oh! You liked that." Wynn's fingers were still in Bexlee. She started to move them around in small motions and her thumb glided up to circle Bexlee's clit.

Bexlee's head fell back and her whole world became Wynn's hand and what it did to her. "Oh, you like this. How about this?" She adjusted a bit, and Bexlee moaned.

"Okay, good to know. What about ... this?"

Wynn shifted her hand back, drawing down Bexlee's undies just enough to expose her clit to the cool air. Then Wynn's mouth descended. She licked and she used her teeth for some gentle stimulation. It was too much. Stars lit Bexlee's vision and she screamed out her orgasm.

When Bexlee returned from her fractured world, Wynn was cuddled next to her. "I'll get my stuff and leave."

"You don't have to go this second. Want to cuddle for a few minutes?"

Bexlee knew it was a horrible idea. Emotions weren't supposed to be part of this. Despite her reservations, she reached for Wynn, securing the other woman's head in the juncture of her arm and chest. She fit perfectly. *Just a few minutes.*

Her phone alarm buzzed. A weight held her down. *Did Stewart crawl into bed with me?* She flung her arm out to grab her phone, but the bed was too big. Suddenly, everything from the night before rushed back. Bexlee cracked open an eye and saw Wynn's head still on her chest. *Oh, fuck!*

She squirmed until she'd managed to get out from under the other woman. She found a door that led to a bathroom. After using the facilities, she splashed water on her face and tried to get her hair in a semblance of order.

Okay, Bex, you need to slip out of here, grab your dress, find your purse, get to the car— preferably dressed—and drive home. Then change quickly and get to work, without being late. Work coffee it is today, as awful as that sludge is. For fuck's sake; today is going to be awful!

With a sigh, she slunk out and found her dress. Her purse was close by. As quietly as she could, she made it to the living room, where she slipped the dress on. She realized she didn't have her shoes and went back for the stupid things.

Back in the common area of the house, she headed for the kitchen. She'd almost made it to the door, when the scent of coffee stopped her. She spun and saw Wynn holding a mug out to her. *How did she always look perfectly beautiful? Is she human?* "Need some go-go juice for the road, Ms. Love-em and Leave-em?"

"It's so early, I didn't want to disturb your sleep." Bexlee blushed as she took the travel mug.

"This is early, but not that bad. I'll probably just get some work done now, and head into the office in an hour. I like being the first in."

Bexlee held up the mug. "Thank you. I need to go change before heading to work."

"Of course."

Bexlee left before they could say anything else. She needed to think about the fourteen or so hours she'd spent with the other woman before she committed to another outing with benefits. Not that the benefits weren't spectacular. She just worried about the rest. She'd had fun last night with Wynn. *Can I keep things light?*

It was early enough that no one else was up at pack house. She ran up to her room, changed, and headed back out. She checked her watch but didn't have time for The Zesty Bean. There would be lines at this time. When she got to the precinct, she ran across the street to the tiny Mom and Pops shop and bought a protein bar and a caffeinated soda. Breakfast of champions.

At her desk, she flopped into her chair, her head landing on her crossed arms laying on a stack of papers she needed to work through.

"Rough weekend, Court?" Cyrus's voice came to her from his desk.

"I don't want to talk about it."

"Of course, you do. Who else do you have? Your brother?" He chuckled. "We could head over to the breakfast shop down the street if you want. It's slow right now. I'm sure it'll be fine. They'll call if they need us."

She perked up at that. "You'll get me breakfast, but I have to spill my secret?"

His face scrunched up. "I was thinking we each buy our own breakfast, but if it means I can pry out your secret, sure, sounds great." He waggled his brows at her.

She groaned, but pushed herself up. "Fine, but no talking before food and coffee."

He laughed as they walked out the door.

The food at the breakfast shop was good. They sat outside and enjoyed the weather. Bexlee was halfway through her omelet when a man walked by. "Why, Cyrus, if you're with a girl, does that make you straight or gay? I can never tell with your kind." He laughed as he continued on his way.

Bexlee's hand shot out to clasp her partner's arm before he could do anything rash. Cyrus just glared at the back of the man who slapped his knee at his own joke. Once he was far enough away, Bexlee turned to Cyrus, whose face had turned to stone. "You okay?"

"No. I mean, I don't care what that ass-wipe says, but I'm not ready to train another partner." Cyrus jerked his arm, trying to get away from Bexlee's hold, but she didn't let go.

"Why would you need a new partner? Are you requesting I be reassigned? Is this because of what that guy said?"

Cyrus's eyes narrowed. "Are you saying you don't want to get away from me now that you heard what he said?"

"I mean, I *could* disregard it as the insane ramblings of an idiot, but if he was saying your trans, what does that matter? You're an excellent cop. And more of a man than most of the men I know, so what's the big deal?"

Cyrus relaxed and Bexlee let go of his arm. "I lost four partners after they found out about me. Three men and a woman. They all thought I was diseased or what I had was catching. Each of them had worked with me long enough that it shouldn't have mattered. I'm just at that point where once my partner learns about me, I assume it's time to move on."

Bexlee gave a one-shoulder shrug. "Well, you worked with four idiots. Even if they were ignorant of who you are as you are now. I mean, you're a man, and if they thought differently, they were idiots. It was their problem, not yours. They should judge you on the work you did, not what's in your pants."

"One of my former partners left the force when they were told switching because they didn't want to work with a trans partner wasn't a good enough reason. The woman said it was for religious reasons. One of the men physically moved. He lives up in Sacramento now. The last was fired when he told another officer about my being trans. I'm not 'out' at work."

"Got it, don't tell the masses ... asses with an 'm.' I can do that."

"You really don't care?" He sounded so small and scared.

"I just can't believe that the others *did* care. But how did that guy know?" Bexlee asked, pointing in the direction the strange guy had wandered off.

"Ah, that was the last guy who got fired for spreading rumors about me. He was told if he told another cop working there, he'd go to jail. He probably believes telling new employees doesn't count."

"Gods above, I'm sorry you had to go through all of that. But, as for what the jerk said, you aren't my type ... I don't date guys."

Cyrus slapped his chest. "I'm heartbroken. Exclusively lesbian then?"

Bexlee shrugged. "I like the ladies."

"Well, for the record, I like the guys. Always have. It's a bit tricky to navigate, but well worth it."

"I bet."

"So, tell me about last night. From how tired you look, I guess you were out with that loan officer?" Cyrus's smile told her he was the kind of cop who missed nothing.

Chapter 16 - All in The Family
Wynn

Tuesday morning Wynn's bed felt cold. *What the hell! You had Bexlee in your bed one night and you're already pining over her? Buck up, the plan was a few encounters to get your wolf happy, that's it.*

She shook herself, then got out of bed to prepare for work.

Korah had taken this week off for a stay-cation. It had been in the books for months, so the office was less enticing. She was a bit miffed that her friend hadn't texted her. She figured there would be some update about her lazing about while Wynn worked. No Meghan, no Korah. All she had to look forward to were her clients, work, and getting away for lunch.

As she drove in, she thought about what she wanted to do with Bexlee next. *I would pull out my straps. I would love to see her tied down and blindfolded. I wonder if she'd go for that.* Wynn had to squeeze her legs together at the thought

The rest of her drive into work, she thought about which of her toys she wanted to bring out to use on the sexy cop. If the woman were tied down, she could bring out her riding crop, or her whip. Maybe punish the punisher. Wynn moaned as she found a parking spot. She wondered if she'd be able to concentrate at all during work.

Not willing to let herself be the only one distracted, she pulled out her phone and texted. Would you let me tie you down and blindfold you?

She knew the other woman would be up and probably at work. Wynn walked over to the coffee shop and ordered her liquid gold and a breakfast sandwich. Waiting for her order to come up, her phone vibrated.

Her pulse jumped before she could pull out the contraption. As long as there was a safe word, yes.

A groan bubbled up from Wynn's gut. She wasn't sure the confirmation was an improvement in her situation.

Once her name was called, she took her food and coffee and headed to the office. Safely alone in her private area, she pulled out her phone and saw there was another message from Bexlee. I'm going to be thinking about this until it happens. I'm not sure if that's good or bad.

Wynn purred. Have you ever been tied down before?

She watched the dots dance as Bexlee typed out her answer. No.

All that time, and that was it? Wynn shook her phone as if that would cause more words to appear. But nothing. Trust me, you'll enjoy it.

The sound of the front door opening let her know she had to stop playing. She sighed. `Later.`
`Just keep imagining all the fun we'll have when you're completely under my power.`

A shot of desire hit Wynn's sex and she slipped her hand in her skirt to relieve the tension. Her touch and the image of Bexlee tied down was enough for a quick release.

She was straightening her outfit when someone knocked on her door.

"Come in."

Sophia opened the door. "Hiya, Wynn. Your morning appointment came in when I opened up. I figured you'd be here. Are you ready for clients?"

"As ready as I'll ever be." She tried to put on a calm air, but worried she looked disheveled.

Leaving her door open, Sophia left and returned with two men.

"This is Tom and Norton, your morning appointment." They looked worn down. Sophia offered them something to drink and headed out with their choices.

Wynn searched their faces. "This is usually a happy time for people. You're about to buy a house! What's wrong?"

Norton's shoulders drooped. "Sorry, we were very excited about this purchase, still are, but last Friday we learned that my mother died suddenly, and we're still in shock."

Wynn reached across and took his hand. "I'm so sorry for your loss. What happened?"

He looked up at her, his drawn face tired-looking. "It was a heart attack. I know she was older, and a heart attack isn't outside the realm of possibilities, but, well, she seemed so healthy."

"Is she in the area?"

Norton nodded. "Yeah. We've been getting everything settled. It's overwhelming. Tom has been my rock. My siblings ... not so much. But none of that is anything you need to worry about. I just don't know why."

Wynn thought she had an idea. Norton had an herbal smell to him. She wondered if he knew he was a witch and that his mom was probably a witch. It usually ran on the maternal side of the family.

Not wanting to focus on the personal, she pivoted the conversation to their future home wants and needs. The meeting continued for another hour. In the end, they agreed to meet again in two weeks.

Once alone, Wynn put in a call to Bexlee.

"Wynn? I'm at work, do you need something?"

She made a fist with her free hand and took a calming breath. Part of her mind wanted to punish the uppity woman, but the other part knew they weren't that couple. *What's wrong with me?* "I just had a client in here, he's a witch, though I have a feeling he doesn't know. His mother died last Friday of a heart attack. I just wanted it to be on your radar."

She heard a grunt. "Do you have a name?"

"I do." They exchanged a bit of information.

"Okay, thank you. I'll look into this. I have stacks of files on my desk, it may already be here." There was a grumble in the other woman's voice.

"You sound stressed."

"No. Well, maybe a bit. I'm at work. It's always a bit stressful, but I'm fine."

Wynn had heard that before. "Do you want to get a drink tonight? Destress ... then, you know, *destress.*"

Bexlee barked out a laugh. "Yeah, sure, I think I would." They made some plans to meet before ending the call.

Wynn leaned back and smiled. She'd head home early today to set up.

Chapter 17 - Dig a Little Deeper
Bexlee

B exlee stared at her phone for what felt like an hour, her pulse hammering in her chest. *Tied down and blindfolded? Gods above.* Her body tensed and if any other werewolf were in the room, they'd smell her arousal. She quickly searched the people around her to make sure no one else saw her phone, what it said, or what she wrote back. *Why does this make me so hot?* She had to respond. As long as there was a safe word, yes.

I can't believe I'm considering this. I barely know the woman, but the idea was to go in and have fun. Someone to fuck around with ... literally. Well, in for a penny and all that.

Bexlee couldn't leave it at that. She wanted to let Wynn know she was interested in playing. With a gulp and another quick search of the room, she dried her palms and her pants and picked up her phone. She followed up her last message with something more encouraging. I'm going to be thinking about this until it happens. I'm not sure if that's good or bad.

Fuck, I have to stop this and get to work!

She put her phone back down and returned to the background check on the same woman who now messed with her thoughts in a very different way.

"Bex, wanna meet in the conference room in an hour to compare notes?" Cyrus yelled from his desk. "I've found out some things, but I'll have it tied down by then."

Bexlee almost spit out her coffee at his wording. "Sounds good, I'll probably have some good notes by then."

Her phone dinged, and she wanted to ignore it, but couldn't. `Have you been tied down before?` She could almost hear Wynn purring this in her ear.

Bexlee started to type. `Never.` She erased it. `I've thought about it but was too afraid to ask my partner.` Nope, not that either, delete, delete, delete. Unable to come up with anything that sounded lighthearted, she settled with a simple. `No.`

Wynn's response came much faster. `Trust me, you'll enjoy it.`

Mouth dry, Bexlee tried to think of something to type, but another text came before her mind could form anything clever. `Later. Just keep imagining all the fun we'll have when you're completely under my power.`

A shot of desire hit Bexlee's sex and she sighed, realizing there was nothing she could do about it.

An hour later, she met Cyrus in the conference room with a stack of files and a pad of paper with a bunch of her notes.

He laughed as she settled and tried to organize it all. "Did you find anything useful in all that?"

She shook her head. "They are the model couple. Married for six years, bought a house, and were about to buy a bigger house because they apparently want kids. They'd applied to be foster parents but were also starting to take meds to help with his potency. They volunteered once a month to feed the homeless."

Nodding, Cyrus shuffled his papers. "That lines up with what I found. They both had clean bills of health, outside his inability to get her pregnant. That inability meant they'd both gone through a lot of medical tests. When I spoke to their doctor, she was surprised about the heart attack. It isn't in either of their family histories, and they're both extremely healthy. She said she'd look into it as a side effect of the pills he's taking, but I stopped her. It was the wife who had the heart attack."

Bexlee's head began to hurt. "None of this makes sense. How can there be an epidemic of heart attacks in town?"

"I tell you, it's magic."

She smiled at her partner. "You know, you almost sound like you believe that."

"I wish I did, it would be so much easier to answer."

Bexlee's phone rang, she saw it was Wynn. Flashing the screen at Cyrus, he smirked. "Answer it."

She sighed, but did. She told her of a client whose mom died of a heart attack. It was a good thing Cyrus couldn't hear the other side of the call, if he heard the bit about being a witch, there'd be a lot of questions to answer.

Once she hung up, she rubbed her temples. "Is there a file from an older woman who died last week? One of Wynn ... um, Ms. Taylor's client's mother died of a heart attack last Friday. She thought the coincidence was odd and wanted to let me know."

Cyrus flipped through his files. "That sounds familiar. Hold on ..." It took him a few moments, but he finally found the file. "I've been given any case that involves a heart attack, and all heart attacks are considered suspect right now. There are just too many. She was in her backyard gardening. Picture of health for a sixty-eight-year-old. I'll push it forward in our cases if you want."

"I'm not sure. They all are probably important. How many of these do we have right now?"

"Fifteen. It's insane. But let's focus on why we're in here. Anything else on the couple from the car on your end?"

Bexlee flipped through her pages. "Do we know anything more about the house they were buying?"

Cyrus let out a long breath. "We do. They were working with Ms. Taylor. Your new friend is popping up over and over. I really don't like coincidences. She's officially on our watch list."

Her gut clenched, but she knew there was nothing she could do about it.

Chapter 18 - What's Your Favorite Thing To Eat?
Wynn

Tonight, they were meeting at a bar. Wynn put on a black leather bra, a tight black miniskirt, and a tight mesh shirt. She didn't wear anything under the skirt. She hoped once Bexlee figured that out, she'd be putty in her hands.

The bar they'd chosen was only a mile from her house, so she decided to walk. Alcohol didn't affect her much, and not having a car would be perfect. The night was nice. She spent the walk planning out what she wanted to do once she had Bexlee back home.

At the bar, she sat on a stool and ordered a margarita; they were half off on Tuesdays. She debated ordering one for Bexlee, but decided she didn't know the other woman well enough and that stunk of "date." *This is not a date. It is an arranged hook-up. That's it. Time to have some fun and get my need for touchy-feely met.*

Wynn didn't have long to wait for Bexlee to arrive. She'd obviously taken the time to go home and change. She wore black silk shorts and a light green tank top. It was tight enough that Wynn could tell she wasn't wearing anything underneath it. Wynn closed her eyes for a moment, enjoying the anticipation tingling throughout her body.

Bexlee took the stool next to hers, put a cool hand on Wynn's knee, and leaned in towards her ear to be heard over the music and other people in the bar. "Nice outfit. I like your top."

Wynn rolled her head to the side so her mouth was next to Bexlee's ear. She put her hand on the other woman's waist and slowly rubbed up until her thumb could play with the side of Bexlee's breast. "I like your top, too, sexy."

A small tremor went through Bexlee as she backed away. She flagged down the bartender and ordered her own margarita.

Once they'd each had some of their cool drink, Wynn leaned in again. "So, do your undies match your bra?"

Bexlee blushed a lovely pink. She then signaled the bartender again. Wynn couldn't hear what she said. Bexlee finished her drink and turned back to Wynn. "Are you asking me if I am here without underwear on?"

Wynn smiled wide. "Well," she reached up and ran the backs of her fingers over the tips of the other woman's nipples. "I can see you're not wearing a bra. I was just wondering if the rest of you was as easily accessible."

She watched as Bexlee shivered at her touch, her nipples hardening. Wynn enjoyed how responsive the cop was to her touch and words. Bexlee licked her lips. "Are *you* wearing underwear?" Her voice was low and husky.

"No, I'm not. What you see is what I'm wearing, nothing more, nothing less."

The spike of desire was thick enough that Wynn was surprised the humans around them couldn't smell it. She leaned in closer. "Do you want to play, Officer?"

Bexlee jumped at a clink of a plate being placed down next to them. She'd ordered a sample of the appetizers, and a second margarita for both of them. She picked up an onion ring and popped it in her mouth. Wynn selected a fried cheese stick then held it up to Bexlee. "What's your favorite thing to eat?"

The other woman shut her eyes and swallowed, her legs pushing together hard. When she opened her eyes, she took a long drink of her margarita. "I don't think they serve my favorite thing to eat here."

"Maybe we should head back to my place? Do you think I have what you want to eat?"

She gulped and nodded. "I do, I really do."

They paid, left a tip, and headed out. Since Bexlee had driven, Wynn slid into her car for the ride back. She noticed a duffle bag in the back. "Planning on spending the night, Officer Court?"

She laughed nervously. "Just covering my bases. I have no expectations."

"Bring the bag in. If you fall asleep, no reason to head home. Smart. But if you leave, then you leave."

Her shoulders dropped as if she worried it would be a friction-point for the night.

There was a parking spot near her house. Once Bexlee parked her small Honda Civic, they got out and headed inside. In the kitchen, Wynn offered her something to drink. "I can mix you something up, but I have some of the best sweet tea this side of the Mississippi. I'm addicted to the stuff, though I usually only drink it when I'm at home."

Bexlee smiled. "Sounds good. I'd love some."

They took their sweet tea into the bedroom and Bexlee froze. There were straps attached to the four corners of the bed. On the table next to the bed lay a whip, riding crop, a selection of vibrators, and a blindfold. Wynn had debated doing more, but decided for this first time, she'd take things slow.

"Okay, safe word How about 'book'? I don't think I'd say that otherwise." Bexlee spoke almost robotically as her focus never wavered from the table of toys.

"Works for me. Now off with your clothes, sexy."

She finally yanked her focus to Wynn and traced her heated attention up and down her body. "What about your clothes?"

"Hmm." Wynn hummed. "If we're going to do this right, you need to follow my directions. And when I tell you to do something, you do it. You say, 'Yes, master.' Or 'Yes, ma'am.' I'm fine with either." Wynn stepped closer to Bexlee and traced a finger down her face. "But when you don't listen to me, I get to punish you." She flicked her finger across one of Bexlee's nipples. The other woman sucked in a quick breath of air.

"Is that what I agreed to?" Bexlee's voice was a mere whisper.

"It is. Are you okay with that?" Wynn knew her eyes burned into Bexlee's. She wanted ... needed her to say yes. She wrapped her hand in the other woman's hair, cupping the back of her head. Her other hand slipped around her waist. They stood a hair's breadth apart.

Bexlee licked her lips and breathed in deeply. Her body leaned towards Wynn as if she craved her. "I don't know if I'm okay with all of this, but I want to be. We have our safe word ... ma'am."

Wynn pulled her in for a searing kiss. She rubbed their bodies together, loving the friction. As quickly as it started, she pushed away. "Okay, strip."

With shaking hands, Bexlee slid off her shorts and shirt. She wasn't wearing anything else.

"On the bed."

She climbed up and sat in the center. Wynn walked over and secured her feet. Her legs would be held wide apart. *The better to eat you with, my dear ...*

Wynn kissed the shin closest to her. "Before I finish, I'll strip. Give you something to think about once I blindfold you." She sashayed around the room, lighting candles and turning on the music. Gyrating her hips, she stripped off her top and then her bra. She rubbed up her torso and squeezed her tits, throwing back her head with a moan.

With a spin, she met Bexlee's eyes, and Bexlee watched Wynn's every move. Her own hands were on her belly. One was inching up, the other down.

Wynn traced down the side of her body to the skirt, still swinging her hips back and forth. She tucked her finger and thumb into the waistband and rotated back a few inches before circling to the front where she unbuttoned and unzipped. The skirt dropped to the floor with a thump. Wynn stepped out of the leather towards the bed, meeting Bexlee's eyes. The other woman was drinking her in.

"Lie down, Bexlee."

"Okay, I mean, yes, ma'am."

Wynn leaned over her to tie the far hand first, her breast landing on Bexlee's face. The other woman's tongue lashed out to play with her nipple. Though Wynn's breathing hitched, she bit back any other sign of her pleasure. She liked that Bexlee had fallen for her trap, now she could find out how much of the game she'd enjoy playing.

Standing up with a blank face, she took Bexlee's other hand, and secured it. Then she selected the riding crop. "Bexlee, did I give you permission to lick my breast? Or to play with yourself while I stripped?"

"Oh! Um. No. Um, no, ma'am ... master?"

"Correct, I did not. That earned you three lashings."

"Lashings?" Her voice got soft as her eyes locked onto the riding crop Wynn had picked up.

Without another word, Wynn snapped the riding crop down on one of her breasts. She cried out, arching from the bed, then moaned. Wynn waited, but she didn't say, 'book.' She snapped the riding crop onto her other breast and Bexlee groaned again. Then she slapped it down right above her sex on her lower belly.

The last left a red mark, and Wynn bent down to kiss the sting away. When she stood back up, Bexlee was watching her wide eyed. "Was that too much?"

Bexlee shook her head. "No ... no ma'am."

Wynn smiled, then gave her a quick kiss. Once done, she placed the blindfold on her. This was a blackout blindfold. Bexlee wouldn't be able to see a thing.

Wynn leaned over and caught a breast in her mouth, sucking hard. She scraped her teeth over the sensitive skin as she backed off. Bexlee's breathing sped up as she took her time investigating the body below her. Using a recently sterilized vibrator, she turned it on, and very slowly, she slipped it inside Bexlee.

Wynn picked up the whip and dragged it over Bexlee's body. It was a small one with a dozen or so strands. She shivered. Wynn flicked it over Bexlee's clit and the other woman cried out, arching up.

"Did you like that?"

"Ya ... yes."

"Hmm, you didn't say ma'am, or master."

Wynn heard her gulp. She picked up the riding crop and flicked it a bit harder on each of Bexlee's breasts. Her head tilted back as she gasped with each contact, her breathing getting erratic.

Wynn climbed on the bed, straddling Bexlee. She leaned down and took each breast into her mouth in turn, licking and sucking the sting away. Then she caught her mouth, exploring it, losing herself in the kiss.

Gods, I could kiss this woman for days. Just leave her strapped to my bed and play.

Pushing up, she said, "I'm going to give you something to eat, just like we discussed at the bar. Are you ready for that?"

Bexlee nodded, then said, "Yes ma'am."

Wynn turned around and straddled her head, lowering herself. When she felt Bexlee's tongue flick out, she groaned from the heat building inside her. She bent and sucked on Bexlee's clit, rolling her tongue, and slowly pulled the vibrator out and pushed it back in, over and over.

Beneath her, Bexlee arched up, growling out her pleasure, giving Wynn more distraction than she'd expected.

Bexlee did something with her tongue and teeth that had Wynn's world fracturing. She called out, trembling atop the other woman. Bexlee screamed out shortly thereafter, arching up. Wynn pulled out the toy and flipped around, lying next to Bexlee. She released one of the other woman's arms and the blindfold. After a few minutes, they got the other restraints off and the blanket up.

In a tired voice, Bexlee said, "I should go home."

Wynn snuggled in closer. "Probably."

Chapter 19 - Scene of The Crime
Bexlee

As quietly as she could, Bexlee gathered her shorts and tank top, found her bag, and went into the guest bathroom. It had a shower, so she figured she could get ready without waking up Wynn. *I can't believe I slept here again.*

I'm such an idiot! But, then again, last night was exciting. Something about giving up control ...

So much of Bexlee's life was about being in control, having a situation in which she wasn't, was almost mind blowing in its own right.

She imagined being tied up again, while the warm water washed away the night's play. *I wonder if that was a one-time thing or if Wynn wants to do it again. Do I want to do it again?*

She dried off, got dressed, and found some semblance of a hair style. Checking her watch, she saw she had time to stop at the café and pick up a sandwich and coffee. *Yes, bringing an overnight bag was much better than slinking home before work.*

The bathroom was closer to the front of the house, but Bexlee still wanted to be quiet. She slowly turned the knob and pushed open the door. The scent of coffee and bacon wound around her like a siren's call, and she moaned.

Collecting her belongings, she made her way to the kitchen to find the delectable sight of Wynn in an all but see-through nighty sitting at the table. There were two plates with bacon, eggs, and toast, and two steaming mugs of coffee. Slack-jawed, Bexlee stared, uncertain what to do next.

"Well, come sit. You do want food before you work, don't you?" There was a twinkle in Wynn's eyes.

Bexlee managed to shut her mouth and nod. "Yes, thank you. You didn't need to do all this. I thought you were asleep."

"I was," she said matter-of-factly. "Then I wasn't." She winked. "I usually get breakfast out, but since I heard you in the shower, I thought, why not. Now, eat, or you'll be late."

"Yes, ma'am." Bexlee froze again, eyes wide, then snorted. The food tasted great. The coffee ... well, it wasn't up to Orin's standard, but it was good. They both focused on eating, not talking.

Bexlee stood once she finished. "Thank you again." She leaned down and kissed Wynn on the cheek. "Can I help with any of the clean up?"

"Gods, no, get to work." She waved her hands in a shooing motion.

Belly full, Bexlee made it to work a few minutes early. She organized her desk by the priorities of the day. When she was barely ready to reach for her first case file, Cyrus flopped down in the chair next to her. "So, how was your date last night?"

"My what now?" She hadn't told anyone she was going out with Wynn.

"Come on, Bex, it's our job to figure things out. You're glowing. Now, that tells me you had a great night. I thought I'd let you tell me versus just telling you, but here you are, forcing me to explain the basics to you, like you're a noob."

Bexlee barked out a laugh. "Fine. I had a lovely night last night, thanks for asking."

"Lovely, huh? Are you even doing it right?"

Thoughts of being tied down, the riding crop's sting followed by the delicious flood of heat and desire, the blindfold, putting her completely in Wynn's world ... she bit back a moan and forced her breathing to stay even. "Yeah, I think so." She nodded.

He laughed and moved to his desk. Before he sat, his phone rang. Bexlee closed her eyes to listen in to both sides.

"Ezra here."

"Homicide. Two dead bodies."

Bexlee stopped listening. The details of where they were going didn't matter. She got her stuff together, and made sure she was ready to go for—"Bex, with me. We ride!"

The ride didn't take long. The house was small and the outside well manicured.

Inside, the two bodies were in the living room, both shot. The gun was near the man's hand. The scent of death and decay nearly choked Bexlee. It was only her time as an officer that saved her from losing her stomach. She had to breathe through her mouth, and she could still taste death.

Bexlee took everything in. "Are we sure this isn't a murder-suicide? That would be my first take on how it looks."

Cyrus's face hardened. "I've told you this before. Never make an assumption at first glance, Court. Follow the clues and evidence. A murderer could place a gun to make it look however he or she wanted. Don't forget that. No 'takes,' got it? When you pre-plan your scene, then you look for the puzzle pieces to fit your assumptions. That doesn't make for a good detective."

Fuck!

"Right, sorry."

"Start over and tell me what you see."

"Two dead bodies. The woman is on the couch under a blanket, shot to the torso, face in shock. The gun is closer to the man, sitting on the chair. Shot under the chin, up through the brain. Honestly, if it isn't murder-suicide, I'd guess the man was shot first to keep him from stopping the murderer. But then I'd expect the blanket to be removed from the woman when she tried to run."

"Okay, get all your thoughts written down. I'll start compiling mine. Forensics will come in with a camera and evidence collecting material."

Gazing around the room, Bexlee's eyes fell on a calendar on the wall. She moved over to it, and her heart stopped. The branding was from Brian Simms Mortgage Lenders, the same place Wynn worked, and last Saturday said, 'Wine with Wynn' in purple letters.

Bracing herself, she slowly took a sniff. Under the cloying scent of blood, death, and decay, she could get a thread of Wynn and her wolf. Wynn had definitely been here.

"Cyrus, I have to leave."

His brows showed his concern as he came over to stand behind her. "Fuck. That's the same Wynn as your Ms. Taylor?" Bexlee nodded. "Well, that puts a wrinkle in this, doesn't it? I'll head out with you; we have enough going on. We'll call in someone else to take this. We were only called in because we're the idiots who work at the ass-crack of dawn. Others will be available. I'll call the chief, go, get to the car."

As she sat and waited, her hands shook. In her soul, she knew Wynn was innocent, but she also knew Wynn was their number one suspect.

Chapter 20 - It's All a Misunderstanding
Wynn

The scent of desire that wafted from Bexlee when she slipped up at breakfast and said, 'Yes ma'am' would carry Wynn through most of the morning. She really enjoyed their bed play and Wynn was convinced she'd be tying the other wolf down again. Maybe she could get out the nipple clamps.

She went to shower and get ready for work. She wondered again about Korah. Her friend usually texted her every few days, and it was Wednesday. Something must be up.

Do I text or do I decide she's having a good time and let her be? If I text I'll have to define this thing with Bexlee because I know she'll get it out of me. Wynn tapped the phone on the palm of her hand and finally decided to wait. If Korah didn't contact her by Friday, she'd call and find out what her friend was doing that was so amazing she'd cut off all communication for days. Hell, Wynn wanted in!

She just finished getting dressed when her phone rang. Figuring Korah had finally called, she answered without checking the display. "Hi!"

"Heya, darlin'. Didn' think you'd be this excited to talk to your old man. Are you packing up to leave that silly coastal city?"

Wynn slumped and rolled her eyes. She didn't have time to deal with her dad's drama. "No, Dad. I'm getting ready for work and need to head out. I don't want to be late. When I answered, I thought it was one of my work friends."

"Now why would a friend call if you're on your way to work? What aren't you telling me, Wynfrey?"

"Gods above, Dad, stop calling me that. The name is awful. Just call me Wynn. And I'm not hiding anything. Korah, my friend, is on vacation. I thought she'd call and tell me how much fun she's having while I toil away at work."

"Ah. Well, I still think you need to get away from that city. You aren't a pack wolf, that isn't how I raised you. You aren't a half-wit bully. Now, get on the computer, find a job in a city without any assholes, and move. It's real simple, Wynn." He deliberately left a pause after her name. "What do you say?"

"I say, I'm going to be late for work. Stop worrying so much about me and all of this. I'm fine."

He scoffed before hanging up.

With a sigh, Wynn gathered her stuff and headed out the door. Though she'd had a filling breakfast with coffee, she still went to The Daily Grind for coffee before heading into her office. Her father had delayed her to the point she wasn't the first to arrive. She raised her cup to Sophia before making her way to her office.

She spared one more thought about Bexlee and their night together. She imagined what they'd do next. *I wonder when I can arrange for our next appointment with benefits?* The thought cheered her as she focused on work.

An hour later, there was a knock on her door. "Ms. Taylor, it's the police."

Doubt and confusion shot through her. *What the hell?* "Come in, the door isn't locked."

Two men in uniform entered. "We need to bring you down to the precinct for questioning. You have the right to remain silent. Anything you say can and will be used against you in a court of law. You have the right to an attorney. If you cannot afford an attorney, one will be provided to you. Do you understand your rights?"

She shook her head. "Am I being arrested? What for?" Her gut twisted in knots. She knew she hadn't done anything, but the idea of police made her nauseous. "I haven't done anything, why would I need a lawyer." Her dad taught her to distrust lawyers as much as she distrusted pack."

"Please follow us, Ms. Taylor, and for now we won't handcuff you. Give us any reason, and we'll use restraint."

Anger flooded her system. She snapped her mouth shut and followed them. Everyone else from the office stood at their door watching, including clients. She was boiling mad.

The ride was quick, and they took her to a small room with a large rectangular table and a mirror. She waved at the mirror and whoever sat on the other side. She hoped they had fun watching. The two men who'd picked her up sat across from her.

"Ms. Taylor, do you know these two people?"

The officer dropped a manila file on the metal table in front of her with a thunk. The taller of the two men slid out two pictures of people—mangled, bloody, and dead. Wynn thought she'd puke. She started to tremble as she gazed at the dead face of her friend and the jerk boyfriend she'd tried to dump weeks earlier.

Desperately hoping this was all a joke, she slid her eyes from the photos up to the gruff officer. "What happened?" She didn't recognize her voice. Small and hollow, begging for an answer that wasn't coming.

"We were hoping you could tell us." His face was hard, demanding, accusing.

"Me? Is this a joke?" She slammed her finger down on one of the photos. "This is my best friend. When I moved to this damned city she was one of the few people who was nice to me. We spend ... oh, gods—" Wynn shut her eyes and covered her face, hot tears stinging her eyes. She tried to hold back her sobs, but her rough breathing told her she failed.

"Please continue, Ms. Taylor."

Her hands dropped to the table, and she made fists, her nails biting into her palms. "Every other Saturday or so we'd have a wine and movie night." She blinked and gave the officers a dead stare. She couldn't believe this was happening. "The man is a piece of work. Her ex-boyfriend. She dumped him after he got physical. He wouldn't take no for an answer. He kept showing up demanding she come back to him. I don't know how he got close enough for this to happen to her."

The smaller officer's head tilted. "Did you do this, Ms. Taylor? Did you kill these two people?"

Her jaw dropped at the pure ridiculousness of the question. "No. I absolutely did not kill my best friend or the asshole she dumped."

If life had been fair, the questioning would be over, but it wasn't. They continued to interrogate her, repeating the same line over and over until she wanted to pull her hair out. In the end, they didn't have anything to hold her on. They released her. They offered to drive her back to her office, but she decided she'd just take a cab, she was done with cops ... all of them.

Where was Bexlee during all this? Leaving me to the jackals.

Back at her office, she got in her car and drove home. The place was dark and locked up. *I wonder what they did about all my appointments?*

All she wanted was a hot bath, and some time alone.

Chapter 21 - Guilty Until Proven Innocent
Bexlee

"**A**re we done here? I've answered these same questions over and over. Are you going to press charges? I will have to change my mind and insist on a lawyer if this is going to continue."

Wynn sounded pissed. Bexlee couldn't blame her. She looked at the text Wynn had sent on her drive to the precinct. `Bexlee, I'm being arrested. Do you know what's happening?`

Despite having an answer, she knew she couldn't reply. Not before the interrogation. It frustrated her. She knew Wynn was innocent, knew it in her gut. She knew the woman, and there was no way she was their suspect, but 'being a werewolf and knowing things' wasn't a good enough reason for her boss. It was one of the most frustrating part of her job.

"I think we're done here. We won't be pressing charges right now, Ms. Taylor, but don't leave town."

She sighed. "I wasn't planning on it. Why would I leave?"

"Do you need help getting back to your car?"

"No, I'll get myself home. Just find Korah's murderer. It'll help if you stop looking at me as your prime suspect." She gave each officer a hard stare as she said it then turned and walked out. Her fierce anger could be felt by non werewolves if Cyrus's exhale next to her was any indication.

Bexlee wanted to follow, but knew she couldn't; she was at work and had to stay.

"I let you watch, Court, but you stay away from this." The chief, sitting between her and Cyrus in the observation room, lashed out at her. "I understand this Taylor woman is a friend. You lay a finger on the case, and it could be thrown out."

"I understand, but she didn't do it."

"Amazing, case closed!" He mocked.

She swallowed her anger. "If you don't mind, I'm going to head home, sir. I'll see you in the morning."

"Sounds good, Court." His demeanor softened a bit as he nodded his approval.

She headed out and got in her car. The guilt at not warning Wynn battled with the reality that she couldn't have. It had been too short a time. Once Wynn's name had been found, cops had been dispatched to pick her up right away. Should she go home? *I could go to Wynn's place. She'd probably kick me out. I don't even know what we are ... friends? Acquaintances? Lovers? Or am I a call in hook-up, ready to meet her needs and drop at a moments notice? I guess that's what I agreed to.* Bexlee sighed.

What would I choose if given the option?

Bexlee didn't want to think about how Wynn had wormed her way into her soul. Easton, Bexlee's non-biological dad, had told her stories of wolves that had bonded quickly. He and her dad had taken months to admit they loved each other, but according to him, for some wolves, it happened fast.

Bexlee never really believed it because in the stories, the couples couldn't survive without each other. She knew that Tamsin's dad followed her mom in death, a tragic love story to the end, but Bexlee had known other couples—like Blake's mom, Joyce—who survived the death of their partner.

As she debated her feelings, she realized she'd driven to Wynn's house. She parked and stared at the small house. *Do I really want to do this?*

She looked at her phone again. Wynn hadn't texted again. *Does she think I abandoned her?* Her heart broke at the thought.

Knowing it was a bad decision, Bexlee got out of the car, walked up to the front door, and rang the doorbell. She waited. She wondered if Wynn would leave her there, waiting.

As she was about to give up, she heard the lock click. The door swung open, and Wynn stood there, standing tall and face hard. "What do you want?"

"To talk."

"You could've texted me before all that happened, you had your chance. It's too late."

"No, I couldn't have. I was never alone. It wasn't an option. They all know I know you. I was being watched."

"What about now? Are you allowed to see me? Or are you here to tell me it's over?"

"I'm here to talk with you. Please, just ... five minutes?"

The door opened wider, but Bexlee heard a snarl. She walked into the kitchen. Wynn shut the door behind her with a resounding click. "Please, Officer Court, sit at the table. Would you like some sweet tea? Coffee? Water?"

Bexlee shut her eyes as Wynn's impersonal words hit like a punch in the gut. "Sweet tea, please." As Wynn turned away, Bexlee rubbed her face. "I'm sorry." Her voice was soft and scratchy. "I told them it wasn't you, but they told me I'm too close. But, I know ... I *know* it wasn't you."

"Why? Because you like how I tie you down and fuck you?"

"No, because ..." She looked up into Wynn's face and her mouth went dry. She wanted to say the rest, but they were words she'd never said. She didn't know how.

A brow shot up on Wynn's face. She placed two glasses of sweet tea on the table and sat across from

Bexlee. She folded her arms across her chest and waited.

Bexlee licked her lips and took a shaky breath. "I'm sorry. You asked something of me I couldn't give you." She dropped her gaze to her hands. She fidgeted with her fingers. "You wanted someone to just hook-up with, nothing more. I should've said 'no.' I thought I could give you that." Slowly, Bexlee met Wynn's eyes, the hazel color turning a stormy green. "I'm falling for you ... hard."

Wynn snorted. "No, you're not. You just like the sex."

Bexlee huffed out a bitter laugh. "I wish that was it. Believe it or not, I've had good sex before. I just haven't fallen for someone before."

Wynn shook her head. "You chose your work over me. Where were you when those men were grilling me? Were you behind the mirror? Eating popcorn? Enjoying the show?"

Bexlee's eyes burned with tears. She hated it when her emotions manifested this way, but she couldn't stop it, all she could do was breathe through it. "I did everything I could."

"I think you should leave. Your five minutes are up." Her voice flat and emotionless.

Bexlee nodded and pushed herself up. "I could love you. Please, don't hate me." She turned and walked out of Wynn's house, her heart cracking.

Chapter 22 - Closed Down
Wynn

The beeps of the alarm tore her from sleep. Wynn usually woke up before her alarm, but today, she hit snooze, rolled over, and was yanked from sleep again by the angry blare of the insistent machine. "Fine! I'll get up!"

She sat up and glared at the restraints and sexy-time toys set up in the corner of the room. Her heart beat faster as she thought about Bexlee. "No, just no. She had a chance, but she chose her job over me."

Tears burned her eyes, but she refused to let them out. She knew she wasn't being fair to the cop, but too much had happened. Meghan and now Korah. Her favorite client ghosted her. What was happening? Why were so many people around her falling?

She wiped her cheeks, wet despite her decision to not cry. *How will I survive a day at work if I'm like this?*

She trudged to the bathroom for a shower. The hot water hid any more tears that may leak out, despite her decision to be strong, as she thought about her friends. Once scrubbed, she pulled on jeans and an old sweatshirt. Finally ready to face the outside world, she checked her phone and saw a text from Brian, her boss.

```
The office is closed today. Too
much has happened, everyone needs
a   day   to   rest.   I'll   see   you
tomorrow. Sorry you had to deal
with     all     that     crap     alone
```

yesterday. Call if you need
anything. -B

With a heavy thump, Wynn dropped onto a
chair in the kitchen. The full day loomed ahead of
her, empty hours needing to be filled. She needed
breakfast and coffee, but beyond that, she didn't
know what she wanted to do. The phone
notifications showed she had other texts. Some
were from Bexlee, but she ignored those. One was
from Silas.

*What does he want? How does he even have
my number?*

Curiosity won out and she opened the message.
Hiya Wynn, it's me, Silas. I know
we don't hang out much, but we were
both friends with Korah. I thought
you might want to get lunch and
have a bitch session.

Staring at the phone, Wynn debated. It would
be nice to get out with someone new and staying
home would be the start of a bad habit. But Silas?
Gah, couldn't it have been literally anyone else?
She looked at her messages and saw the slew of
messages from Bexlee. Well, besides Bexlee?

Wynn got up and turned on the coffee maker.
In the freezer she found some frozen breakfast
sandwiches she put in the toaster oven. Once she

had some food and caffeine, she considered Silas's offer.

What can it hurt? He could become a friend ... right?

Wrinkling her nose at her phone, she pulled up Silas's text and replied. Sounds great, what time? Where do you want to go?

She was amazed how quickly his response came. He must have been waiting. *Or have as little to do today as I do.* They agreed on a time and place. She went into the living room, grabbed the remote, and turned on some trashy TV. She had some time to kill, and didn't need anything absorbing to fill it.

Two hours later, the hostess led Wynn to a table in the courtyard of a cafe. Silas was already there waiting for her. Looking like he'd walked off the cover of a magazine, he stood as she approached. He wore fitted dark wine slacks and a black button-down with a geometric design in a color that matched his pants. Even his short brown hair was styled perfectly.

As she approached, his eyes traveled her body in her jeans and old sweatshirt and his fixed smile faltered for a second before widening.

She never left in something this frumpy, but she didn't care today.

He lifted his hand to grasp hers, though his handshake was as limp as a dead fish. She resisted shivering. "Wynn, I'm glad you could make it. All of this is so hard."

Wynn dropped into the seat opposite him. "I just can't believe this is happening. Meghan with her heart attack, Korah with this ... gods ... I don't even know what to call this. It's ugly."

Silas tilted his head. "I don't know what to call it either. I heard from Brian that she was found at home dead with that ex-boyfriend of hers, but that's all the police are releasing." His eyes lit up, boring into hers.

She slumped, suppressing a scowl. *He just wants gossip.*

She shook her head and shrugged. "I'm not sure what happened."

"Did the cops tell you anything when they pulled you in? Was it natural causes? Murder? They're playing this one close to their chest."

The waitress came over and Wynn ordered a chicken sandwich and veggies. She wanted a cheeseburger and fries, but Silas ordered a salad, and she didn't want to order more than him. He always looked down at her with a judgmental sneer, she didn't want to add to his opinions on her food choices. She could get a burger on the way home. *Why did I even come out to meet him on my day off? What a waste of free time.*

"Do you know if Brian is going to do something for Korah? Is there going to be a memorial at the company?"

Silas leaned back at Wynn's change of subject and raised an eyebrow. "I think so. This situation seems bigger than what happened to Meghan, not only in severity, but because we've lost two people this month. We don't want clients to think our company is cursed."

The food came as he spoke. Like Silas, she wore fashionable clothes, a fitted black dress with lace cuffed sleeves and a belt. The more Wynn looked around, the more she realized she should've cared about her outfit.

Wynn cut up her chicken before taking a bite. She washed it down with a sip of wine. "I hadn't thought about that. If people realize we've lost two of our loan officers, they may go somewhere else. At least we have several realtors who work with us.

They'll know better." Her head started to hurt. This was getting to be so much worse.

"That's true." Silas's focus landed on someone behind her, his face lightening up with a genuine smile. "Sweety, you made it!"

Wynn turned around. A man walked up to them, tall, lithe, with ash-brown curly hair. Short facial hair framed the lower half of his face. His blue eyes looked like the sky before a storm. Dark gray with a shot of blue in the center. He wore a pale green shirt the color of leaves on a spring day. The shirt molded to his sculpted frame and was tucked into dark black pants. Everything about him screamed 'designer' and 'expensive.' If Silas looked good, this man had every person, man and woman, in the café stunned.

Silas stood and the two embraced. Even Wynn, who strictly liked women, found the image of the two of them intriguing.

Silas pulled away. "Wynn, this is Loui. Loui, my work friend Wynn."

Wynn stood and shook his hand. He had a strange scent about him. *Is he wearing cologne? I can usually suss out the base chemicals, but this one smells awful.* She placed it as old leather. Checking his outfit again, she realized his belt and shoes matched, and were leather. Expensive, everything about him was expensive. She smiled. "Nice to meet you."

They sat and Loui took a bite of Silas's salad. "I've heard all about you, Wynn. New to the state, alone here, no pack of your own."

Her heart skipped at the word 'pack'. The innocent look he gave her made her realize the word was just a random one he'd used. She scrunched her face, confused. "What?"

"You know, family all back where you came from."

Okay, this guy must be as foreign to California as me with the way he talks, but how dare he assume about me! "I have friends here." She realized she had a bit too much edge to her voice.

He put up his hands towards her, palms up. "No offense. I just know moving to a new city can be hard. I'm glad you've found people here to call your own."

She took a bite of her sandwich. It was good, even if it didn't hit the spot as well as a burger would've. "Are you from around here?"

He laughed. "No, I'm from out east. I came here about a year ago. I got a job at a local chemistry company."

Her head nearly stopped working. *He's a chemist? I was convinced he was a model, like all of Silas's other boy-toys! Pretty and smart? No way.* Wynn worked to keep herself from shaking her head.

His eyes lit up. "I know, right? Everyone assumed I moved here for a modeling career or acting, but no, I actually have a brain."

Amusement bubbled in her. *What is he doing with Silas? I think I could like this Loui guy.*

Wynn didn't often misread people as poorly as she had Loui. They spent the rest of the meal discussing his work and telling stories of Meghan and Korah. Wynn still felt checked out, but the meal ended a lot differently than she'd expected.

Chapter 23 - Missing Wolves
Tamsin

Tamsin sat at her desk in the office of the alpha suite, looking over the plans for the remainder of the quarter. This was her first year teaching college and the idea of the quarter ending before winter break thrilled her.

Paige came up and rubbed her shoulders. "You're growling at that paper, Tam. What could it possibly have done to deserve such ire?"

She relaxed and leaned into the other woman's hands. "I'm just adjusting to teaching quarters and not semesters. Thanksgiving is in a week, and several students emailed me that other teachers set online assignments. They tell me I'm the only class that's still being held. It's ridiculous."

"Look, it's Thursday, you have the weekend to scowl at that paper. Let's go to the kitchen and have dinner. It smells done." Paige turned the notebook over that Tamsin was using for her planning.

She grumbled, but stood up and followed the lovely woman towards the food. "Is that melted cheese I smell?"

From the kitchen, she heard Orin say, "Baked mac and cheese."

Tamsin entered the kitchen. "Lobster mac?"

He rolled his eyes. "Never good enough."

Laughing, she sat at the table and looked at her pack with pride. At the big table sat Orin, Paige, Toby, Easton, Dylan and Georgette. Sitting at the kids' table with Stewart and Rainy were Bexlee, Joyce, Jolly, and Timothy. Her pack had come so far from the four she'd found when she'd beaten Vernon.

"Your food is always delicious, an alpha can always hope, you know."

Orin winked. "Next time buy me some lobstah!"

She closed her eyes to read her connection to all her wolves. As alpha, she received a lot of information from each of her pack mates. She blocked the extra stimulus on a daily basis to keep herself from becoming overwhelmed but tried to check in regularly.

All her focus landed on the kids' table.

"Most of the kids liked my dress today, Aunt Bex, but there's a girl who said I shouldn't be wearing it." Stewart stared at his hands as he spoke.

Next to him, Rainy's face hardened. "You should ignore Ashley, she's mean. She picks on everyone, and the teacher doesn't do anything about it."

Bexlee rubbed her nephew's arm. "Do you like to wear Rainy's old dresses?"

He slowly looked up at her, his lower lip caught in his teeth. He nodded.

Her hand stopped and squeezed. "Then that's all that matters, Stew. You need to be the person you want to be. People like this Ashley, they will always find reasons to try to bring other people down. If it wasn't your dress, it would be your bookbag, or your hair. It doesn't matter what you do, they just need a reason to bring others down so they can feel bigger."

Stewart's face screwed up. "But why?"

"I don't know. I've never understood this attitude. I just know that you are an amazing kid. You should be like a stone in the river and let her words flow over you. You are beautiful and her words mean nothing in the bigger river of life."

Tamsin wasn't sure if that metaphor made sense, but Stewart smiled and started eating his dinner. Despite the boy's better mood, Tamsin realized, through their bonds, that Bexlee was still upset. Digging deeper, she knew her mood didn't have anything to do with elementary school antics.

Joyce, sitting on Rainy's other side, looked over to the adults' table. "Where is my daughter? Does anyone know where Blake and Maria are?"

Orin whipped his head around as if they'd suddenly show up. Georgette smiled slyly.

Next to Tamsin, Paige leaned forward. "What do you know?"

Georgette shrugged. "Maria texted me this morning saying she wouldn't be going in to work with me and to not worry. I'm guessing she and Blake took a long weekend together."

Joyce narrowed her eyes. "If they eloped, I'm going to kill them."

Chapter 24 - A Walk in The Park
Bexlee

I *wonder if I could go to Stewart's school in my uniform and scare this five-year-old Ashley ... would it be crossing a line? Probably. Yeah ... probably. Maybe I'll ask Cyrus.* She smiled at the thought of Cyrus glaring down at a kindergartener.

"That doesn't look like the nicest smile. What mischief are you getting into, my friend?"

Bexlee snapped out of her thoughts and gazed up at Tamsin. "Nothing you'd approve of, trust me."

Her alpha raised an elegant eyebrow. "Oh, I don't know. Why do I feel it has something to do with a cop's uniform and a misbehaving five-year-old girl."

Heat rose up Bexlee's chest to her face. She ducked to hide her embarrassment. Terrorizing a kid wasn't a laudable thing to think about.

A hand landed on her shoulder. "Can we go take a walk?"

Swallowing her shame, she nodded. "Yes, alpha." Her voice came out soft with all the self-doubt that had plagued her since the last visit she'd had with Wynn.

Outside a soft breeze rustled the leaves in their yard. Tamsin led her to the park near their house and to one of the walking paths that, at times, skirted near their running path. A few other people were out in the nice weather, enjoying a hike, but for the most part they were peacefully alone, something they did get with the pack around.

They walked silently for a few minutes. Bexlee enjoyed the scent of eucalyptus, a gentler aroma in her human form. Off to the right she spied one of the pesky feral cats, and a small smile forced its way on her face.

Tamsin rubbed down her arm from shoulder to wrist. "What weighs so heavily on you, Bexlee? You were filled with these emotions before your talk with Stewart."

A boulder punched her in the chest. She didn't want to think about the last day—much less talk about it—but what choice did she have? She had to talk to someone and who better than her alpha. She squeezed her eyes shut as if in an effort to hold back the tsunami of conflicting emotions threatening to sweep her away.

Stopping, she hugged her arms around herself. "It was supposed to be emotion-free. A way for her to get her physical needs met ... mine, too. It wasn't supposed to be more. I wasn't supposed to be more!" Her voice rose as she repeated herself. "I broke the rules." Her eyes stung, and as she wiped them she realized her cheeks were wet. *Am I crying? Holy hells, I'm crying.*

Tamsin pulled her into a hug. "Sometimes, when our mind, body, and soul tells us it's just a fling, a way to pass time from point A to point B, our wolf has a different plan for us."

"But it was only—" Bexlee sniffed, trying to get air, "—my wolf. Her wolf doesn't care about me. Or us." Bexlee felt her heart breaking all over again. How could she have gotten herself into this situation? "I don't know what to do."

As she cried, she felt herself calm, safe in her alpha's arms. Tamsin rubbed her head and she relaxed more. She began to feel she may survive this, even if Wynn refused to see her again.

"You'll lean on your pack; let us help you. You aren't alone, Bex. Focus on your day to day, helping Stewart, helping around the house, and getting things done at work."

Bexlee pulled back and sniffled. "Yeah, okay, that makes sense. I can do that."

Tamsin smiled at her warmly. "How is work going?"

"There are so many of these heart attack cases. My partner jokes that it feels like magic. It has to be black witches, why are they being so obvious?" A snarl roughened Bexlee's voice. "And then they're targeting Wynn—they have to be. So many people around her are going down, I can't figure it any other way. And one of her friends was involved in a murder-suicide. I can't figure out whether it was the black witches, or if it's coincidence, but it's so frustrating."

Tasmin took her hand and gave it a squeeze before tugging her along as she resumed their walk. "It could be completely random, but with the way black witches work, it could also be targeted. Wynn is the person you had the arrangement with?"

Bexlee slumped. "Yeah."

"I don't blame you; she's gorgeous. She also needs people. I'm glad she found you. She needs to know about all this. If you think she wouldn't listen to you, I can contact her."

"No." The thought of someone else talking about this with Wynn stunk of cowardice. "I'll do it. I'll find a way to get a hold of her."

"Okay, just make sure she understands how black witches work. It's a matter of safety. There's also the fact that, once she understands us better, perhaps she'd consider the safety of joining the pack."

Bexlee rubbed her temples. *I wonder how hard it will be to get that stubborn wolf to speak with me again. Herding cats would probably be easier.*

Chapter 25 - Bad Luck
Wynn

Friday morning Wynn didn't want to go to work. She didn't want to face an office with a third of the people dead and gone. Especially when the third represented her friends. Part of her wondered if she would be next.

She picked up her phone and saw the texts from Bexlee. They started on Wednesday.

`I'm sorry I didn't warn you, I couldn't. I was always with another officer. Please, let me explain.`

Wynn scowled at the message. Of course, she could've found a way. Sending off a quick text wouldn't have been that hard, would it've been?

Later that day, before she'd shown up on Wynn's doorstep there was another text. `I don't want this to be the end. Can we talk?`

`Please?`

She still wasn't sure if letting Bexlee in had been the right decision or not. Their talk hadn't been at all productive on either side. Bexlee just blathered on, not saying anything new.

Thursday the woman had sent: `I shouldn't have said what I said. The arrangement was no strings attached. I brought feelings into the picture. Forgive me.`

Damn straight it had been out of line. She had feelings for Wynn. What the fuck was that? This was about hook-ups. A way for Wynn to meet her wolf's need for physical contact—that was it. How

155

dare Bexlee bring in more than that! Wynn snarled a profanity under her breath.

Later that evening came: I know you're done with me. I can't change your mind, but I have something important I need to tell you. If not me, then Tamsin or another one of the others in the group. It's ... please, can we talk?

This sounded different. *I'll give myself an hour to think about what could be so important that Bexlee would feel she needs to speak to me.*

She switched over to her messages with Sophie, the office secretary. I'm going to take today off. No. One day wasn't enough. She changed it to: I'll be in on Monday. *Even the week of Thanksgiving will have work for me to do.*

She hadn't expected a response for a bit, but Sophie's reply came right away. Good. Find someone to grieve with. Don't be alone. I'll see you next week.

She got up and slipped into a loose, knee-length, pale orange skirt and a cream blouse. In the kitchen she made herself an omelet and coffee. After considering her day, she pulled out her phone and texted Bexlee back. If you're available for lunch, I can meet you then for this talk of yours. Otherwise dinner. I took the day off, so I have time. Her thumb hovered over the send before she added. Don't read too much into this.

She decided to head out to take a walk. She wasn't sure where she was going, she just needed to move.

Could Korah's death be connected to the others? Does that even make sense? Can a murder and a heart attack be connected?

She rounded a corner and the scent of freshly made waffle cones hit her. *That's just what I need!* She entered the store and ordered a waffle bowl with s'mores ice cream. Sitting outside, she thought about why Korah would've allowed Jerry into her house. She wouldn't've. Unless he demanded something of his he'd left at her house. She may have fallen for that.

Her hand drifted down, and she touched paper. Someone had left a newspaper on the seat next to her. She snorted at something so old fashioned. *People still print and sell these things?*

She opened it up and paged through the different articles. Her phone beeped. Bexlee had responded, requesting dinner. Her gut clenched, but she squashed any feelings of anticipation. *This is about business, that's it!* She quickly sent off a time and place.

As she flipped through the pages of the newspaper, enjoying her chocolate ice cream with marshmallow swirl and graham cracker crumble, her heart stopped at an article.

Local couple dies in a car crash. Tonya Wilde, 28, had a heart attack early Wednesday morning on her way to work. In the head-on collision, both she and her husband, Josh Wilde, died. The driver of the other car is in critical condition, but is expected to survive ...

Wynn stopped looking over the paper, unable to believe what she read. It felt like her heart stopped beating. Her favorite clients hadn't ghosted her, they were dead. Another victim of the heart attacks happening all over town. First Meghan, and now them. *Everyone I care for ...*

Am I bad luck? What if they go after Bexlee because of me? The thought of Bexlee found dead sent a cold knife to her heart.

Wynn crumpled the paper and tossed it in the recycling bin. *No! She's just a fucking hook-up!*

Chapter 26 - Breaking My Heart
Bexlee

Bexlee's mind wouldn't stop torturing her. She didn't sleep well the night before and now her thinking was fuzzy. It was her third large coffee, and her body trembled with its need for sleep.

The chief's voice snapped out, filling the room with its command. "Court, Ezra, to my office." Bleary eyed, Bexlee pushed up from her desk, grabbed a pad of paper, a pen, and slogged to the one private office in the building, following closely on Cyrus's tail. They sat in the seats facing their boss. Cyrus took the lead. "What's up, boss. Letting us go early since it's Friday?" He chuckled at his own joke.

The chief stared at them blankly. He pushed a folder at each of them. "This just came in. Since the suspect is familiar to you, I wanted you to understand, it's still need-to-know, so it shouldn't leave this office. We've kept this out of the news. We figure it will show in tomorrow's paper, but until then, we still have some freedom without reporters."

Bexlee opened the folder. She skimmed the reports. The double murder from the following weekend was a murder-suicide, as it had appeared. There was gunshot residue on the man's hand and the gun was registered to him. The interviews with friends and family painted a picture. She'd broken up with him and he'd continued to harass her. It followed everything Wynn had said during her interrogation.

The previous night, Bexlee had sat down with Orin, Joyce, Tamsin, and Jolly. They'd talked about South Dakota and the pack that had been targeted almost forty years ago. Black witches had come in and set a spell that caused weird accidents. Everything seemed like simple coincidences, but when put together, it wiped out a witches' coven and almost destroyed a wolf pack.

This report looked above-board, but was it? With it being another person connected to Brian Simms Mortgage Lenders, was it planned or random? Could it all be connected?

Bexlee met the chief's piercing gaze. He seemed to be able to see into a person and read more than they wanted to reveal. She closed the file and wiggled it. "Thank you for sharing this. Can I let Ms. Taylor know, or is it classified?"

His eyes narrowed. "You can let her know if you are certain it goes no further than her." His brow rose. "If there's a chance she'll talk, then keep this to yourself." He paused to examine her, as if he was reading her intentions. "Make sure she knows about the confidentiality of the situation. If we find out she's spoken to the media, then we have an issue on our hands."

"Understood, sir."

When Bexlee got back to her desk, Wynn had finally texted her back. She wasn't sure which text had worked its magic, but Wynn offered lunch or dinner. Bexlee asked about dinner, not thinking she could take time away from the middle of her day.

The rest of her shift, she and Cyrus compiled notes on the heart attack victims. One of the forensics experts found a promising lead in a chemical that occurred in all the victims. This may have been the break in the case they were hoping for, but the report was preliminary, and it would take a few days for the big brains to figure it out.

Bexlee left work, headed home, and changed. She decided on tight, dark jeans and a form-fitting black t-shirt. *This isn't a date; I'm going for comfort.*

When she arrived at the restaurant—Burgers By the Bay—she saw Wynn sitting at a table in the corner and went to sit with her. She sat, and they sat in an awkward silence until the waitress came and she ordered a double bacon cheeseburger with fries.

The two sat in silence while they waited for their food. The air of tension and awkwardness grew, making Bexlee's skin itch. She didn't want to scratch, but she couldn't help fidgeting, folding and unfolding the napkin.

After the food arrived, and they'd each taken a few bites, Wynn's face scrunched up. "Why are we here, Bexlee? What did you want to talk about?"

A lump formed in her gut. "I have a story to tell you."

"What if I don't want to hear a story? What is this about, Officer Court?"

"Please, just hear me out. It started in South Dakota years ago." She explained what she knew. "I don't know how much of what's happening is connected to the black witches, but I have my guess. Their spells are like a computer viruses. They slowly permeate an area, working their way through. I don't know how much they work to ensure it does what they want it to do or if they specifically target people, but my gut says they do both."

"But why me?"

"I don't know." Bexlee shrugged. "I also don't know if it's you, specifically—or your company."

Wynn started ticking items off on her fingers. "Meghan, Korah, my clients. That's three. All connected to me. It feels personal."

"True, but I read the reports. Everyone at the office said Korah was good friends with Silas and that she and Jael used to date. Then there was the fact that Meghan and Brian fought over company policy. She also disagreed with both Silas and Jael.

And, from what I understand, Jael dated her, too. He seemed to get around. As for Mr. and Mrs. Wilde, they were your clients, but the first time around, five years ago, they were Silas's. Your whole office is very close-knit."

Wynn's face hardened. "So, you're saying I'm overreacting?"

"No." She looked around to make sure no one was listening. "You're a werewolf. I'm saying you're not. I just think we need to figure out how this witch figured out who you were and why they targeted you. Or who in your office pissed the witch off. There's been a lot of heart attacks—not just the ones around you."

They each focused on their food while at least Bexlee thought about what had been said. Finally, Wynn asked, "What about my being the prime suspect in Korah's murder?"

Bexlee felt another ice dagger. Every one of these items Wynn brought up was a reason they were no longer playing.

She spent a few minutes ensuring Wynn understood that what she was telling her was confidential, but being a wolf, secrecy was second nature to them. She then let Wynn know she was no longer being investigated as a prime suspect.

When the meal was done, Bexlee threw some money on the table. Then she caught Wynn's gaze. "Do you need some touch therapy?"

Wynn raised an eyebrow, crossed her arms, and leaned back in her seat. "You're not spending the night."

"I know. That wasn't the question." She held herself still, face blank. Inside she quivered.

"Yes, fine, but you'll do what I say and how I say it. And then, you'll leave. Do you understand?"

"Yes."

They each went to their respective cars and drove to Wynn's house. Bexlee wasn't sure why she offered herself up like this, except she cared for the other woman, and didn't want her need for physical contact to go unmet. Bexlee had the pack, and two kids to wrestle with, and hugs and small touches from the others. Wynn had nothing. Except this.

Once they arrived, Wynn marched them to her room. "Strip. Get up on the bed. I'm going to tie you down again. This is about me, not you."

Bexlee did as she was told. Wynn pulled the straps tighter than last time. Despite what Bexlee expected, heat built between her legs and her breathing grew rough.

Wynn attached straps around her legs and lower abdomen, then fidgeted with something at her waist pressing down on her sex. She tried to see, but couldn't past the waterfall of hair. Then Wynn moved and she saw a large dildo sticking up from between her legs. Before her mind could comprehend what she saw, Wynn placed a blindfold on her.

There was a click, and the dildo, placed just above her clit, began to vibrate. She bit back a moan as heat built in her. "Now, Bexlee, I'm going to ride you until I'm good and satisfied. I may decide I want to come twice, we'll see. The night is young. I'll leave you strapped down until I'm fully pleasured. Do you understand?"

Bexlee nodded, uncertain of the rules and distracted by the vibration low and intense on her body.

A crisp sting assaulted her breast and the crack from the slap echoed in the room. She gasped.

"What was that?" Wynn asked.

"Yes, ma'am."

Another slap to her other breast, harder than last time. Bexlee's body boiled with heat. The pain shot right to her sex.

"I only want to hear you call me 'master' tonight."

With a quaver to her voice, Bexlee managed to say, "Yes, master."

The moist warmth of Wynn's mouth sucked in one of her breasts, and her tongue flicking over the nipple made Bexlee shiver. Wynn's hand rubbed the other one. Bexlee arched into the sensation.

Suddenly, Wynn stopped, and each nipple received a stinging slap with whatever she'd been using. "Did I say you could move? This is about me, not you. If you get pleasure, be happy, but only move if given permission." Another slap to each nipple.

Bexlee yelped with the pain, then breathed out, "Yes, master."

The bed dipped and then Wynn's weight was over Bexlee's waist. She moved up. "I'm going to scoot to your face, and I want you to lick me to orgasm. Then I'll play with that toy strapped onto you."

"Yes, master."

She was careful of Bexlee's arms as she positioned herself, then lowered herself down. Not having hands to use made the process hard. Not being able to see made it even more difficult. But Bexlee flicked her tongue and sucked. She probed her tongue in when Wynn arched forward.

Bexlee lost herself in the meal presented to her, licking, sucking, flicking, nibbling. Eventually she heard Wynn cry out and pull away. Bexlee almost came with the other woman's moans and release. Wynn scooted down and sucked Bexlee's breast. She felt the pressure on the strap on and guessed she slipped down onto it.

Wynn set a slow rhythm, moving up, pumping herself on the dildo, its vibrations rubbed Bexlee, as well. Wynn shifted to kissing her, demanding her mouth in a deep kiss as her motions got faster.

The pleasure built in Bexlee until she couldn't control herself; she bucked up, her body meeting Wynn's, and screamed, electrified with the orgasm.

When she came down, with small aftershocks of sensation, Wynn continued to ride her, the pain of the vibrator against her clit almost too much.

"Are you back with me, cop?"

Bexlee tried to speak, but her body was still reeling from ... everything. She nodded, unable to get words out. The biting pain of the lash on her breasts brought her back to the present.

"I asked you a question."

"Yes, master, I'm back."

"Well, then" Another set of slaps, this time to her hips. "That's for orgasming without permission." Two more to her inner thighs. Bexlee didn't know if her body could take it. "And this is for moving without permission."

Wynn continued to use her body. She tried to get Bexlee to orgasm again, but this time Bexlee asked permission. She was denied. With a groan, she tried to hold back. As if aware of her struggle, Wynn pushed her.

"Please, master, can I come?"

"No."

Bexlee lay there, her body electric with need. Wynn screamed out her pleasure and collapsed on top of her. When her mouth touched Bexlee's ear, she whispered, "Now. Scream for me, cop." Then she licked and nibbled the ear. That was all it took to send Bexlee crashing over the edge.

Boneless, unsure she could think,—much less move—Bexlee reeled from the orgasm.

Wynn rolled away from her.

Bexlee heard the restraints being unfastened, before she felt the tension relax from her limbs. "You can leave now, Officer Court."

Chapter 27 - I'm Totally Sober, Ms. Officer Wynn

Saturday afternoon, Wynn took a run by the beach. She had to think about everything that had happened over the last week. A week ago, she was at Korah's house, drinking port wine, and gossiping about their lives. A week ago, she was sad about the sudden death of a friend in a crazy, fluke heart attack. A week ago, the biggest worry she had was being a lone wolf in a city containing pack wolves.

Today? A week later? Black witches. Her mind whirled with what Bexlee had told her. She'd tried sex therapy, one of her favorites, but to no avail. It had let her get some actual sleep, but that's about it. She felt guilty for using Bexlee ... guilty. She'd never felt guilt as part of her sex games before.

But Bexlee enjoyed herself, I'm sure of it.

Wynn's thoughts took on the cadence of her footfalls as she ran. *Even if I got a bit rough in her punishments and left her skin a bit red, I could smell her desire spike every time.* The more Wynn thought of the games they played, the more she wished she had the other woman there. She didn't mind a bit of public displays.

I wonder if she'd fuck me on the beach? She clenched her fists together, digging her nails into her palms. *Stop it, Wynn. You can't play with her anymore. It isn't fair, not if you can't reciprocate her feelings.*

Sadness washed through her as gray as the ocean under the cloudy sky. She didn't want to give up her time with Bexlee. *But I'm not developing feelings for her, I'm just getting used to having someone around ... that's all it is.*

She narrowed her eyes and forced herself to think about something else. Next week was Thanksgiving. She had a couple of days to decide if she'd go home to Kentucky or stay here and spend the feast day alone. In the past, she'd spent it with Korah, but that wasn't an option this year. *I will not cry.* She blinked back the pins and prickles that came to her eyes.

Gods above, spending it in Kentucky sounds like hell. Dad and my cousins? I finally escaped them. I have to have more people around here I can enjoy a meal with. Or I'll order food and spend the time alone. Or maybe Bexlee would want to spend some time playing.

She realized where her mind had gone and stopped running. *For fuck's sake, I need to get control of myself!*

She saw a bar up the road and jogged to it. Her watch read three, but it was happy hour somewhere. She ordered onion rings and two gin and tonics. She wanted to not feel and accomplishing that would take more than one drink.

She shot the first one back and started in on the second. It was gone by the time the onion rings came, so she ordered a third.

"Does the third want a friend like the first two?" the bartender joked.

With a small shrug, Wynn agreed. "Wouldn't hurt. I didn't drive, and my drinks don't like to be lonely."

She tried to order two more, but it'd been less than an hour, and he cut her off. She paid and started to walk home. She saw another bar down the beach and made the same order, replacing the onion rings with mini tacos. She was cut off after four drinks again. As she walked out, the world tilted a bit, and she thought this time, the bartender may have been correct.

She walked onto the beach. It was off the main drag, and in November, empty. Another tilt of the world, *someone really should look into that*, and she decided to plop down in the soft sand.

She pulled out her phone and started playing with it. When it started to ring, she forgot what she was supposed to do. Her heart beat faster and she stared at it, dumbfounded.

"Hello?"

Wynn didn't know what to do, she forgot that the blasted contraption was used to talk to people in real time. Should she hang up?

"Wynn? Are you there? Is everything okay?"

She slumped; she couldn't hang up. It would send the wrong message. *No, it would send the right message, but I can't send that message, I've already been too mean.*

"I'm pine."

"You're what?"

"Mine. No, line. What? Wait? What did you ask me?" She giggled, then slapped a hand over her mouth. *I don't laugh like that!*

"Wynn, are you at home?"

"Bexlee? Is that you?"

There was a sigh, which confused Wynn. Was Bexlee okay? "Where are you, Wynn?"

"Oh, a beach ... pretty now ... like you, you're pretty, too." She chuckled again and slumped, resigned to the noises she was making.

The line was silent for a moment and Wynn forgot why she was holding her phone to her ear. She carefully lowered her hand and looked at the device. Bexlee's name was on the display. Why was Bexlee calling her? She put the phone to her ear. "What do you want Bexlee?"

"You called me ... no, forget it, never mind. Nothing, Wynn, I don't want a thing."

Her words cut through Wynn's soul, and made her want to cry. Her voice came out small. "Nothing?"

"You're drunk, Wynn. We can talk when you're sober."

"You're pretty. I like you, Bexlee."

"Gods, I wish that were true. I'm going to go. Can you get home?"

Wynn looked around. "The water is pretty, Bexlee, like you."

Sitting back, Wynn almost fell. She put her hands back and caught herself. After a few moments she thought she heard a voice, but there wasn't anyone else at the beach, so she realized that couldn't be the case. She watched the gray water move under the clouds, soothed by the sound of the surf against the beach.

There were birds that flew by, and the sky got a bit darker, but all in all, it was the most at peace she'd felt in a long time. Her mind was blissfully blank as she sat there watching the ocean lap in and lap out.

A crunching noise came from behind her. She looked over her shoulder and saw Bexlee walking towards her. A light happiness blossomed in her as the other woman walked up, then sat down next to her. "You okay?"

"I'm amazing. Why? Are you okay?"

"Not really. You called, then just stopped talking. You're drunk. I was worried about you. Since you left the connection open, I had a cop friend track your phone down. It was the only way I could find you."

"Will you be in trouble?" She focused to get the words out.

"No, but even if it got me in trouble, I'd've done it. You're more important than a reprimand on my record."

Wynn was sobering up. She knew what she'd done and said. She thought about whether she regretted any of it, and decided she didn't. "So, what now?"

"I help you get home, then I'll do what you want me to do."

Wynn shifted to gaze out at the ocean, pondering Bexlee's willingness to be what it was she needed ... do what she asked. "What if I want you to stay?"

"Then I'll stay."

Chapter 28 - Good Morning Sunshine
Bexlee

Back tight, Bexlee stretched and yawned. She tried to shift position and ended up rolling off the couch with a thud.

"Ouch." She said the word softly, not wanting to wake up Wynn. The clock on the mantle said six-eleven. "Gods, it's early for a Sunday ... not worth trying for more sleep, though ... good enough."

Every bit of her body ached. This was not a sleeping couch, with its stiff cushions and cardboard-feeling pillows ... designer pillows. *I should've checked out Wynn's bed. I bet she has extra pillows that are better than these awful ones.*

With more effort than she wanted to admit, Bexlee pushed herself to her feet and trudged to the bathroom. After using the facilities, she washed her hands, then turned the water to cold. She splashed her face until the chill fully woke her up.

What am I even doing here? Once Wynn realizes I spent the night, she's going to kick me out. I should've just gone home last night and gotten a decent night's sleep. But, on the other hand, she asked me to stay. Is there any possibility that a sober Wynn will agree with a drunk Wynn?

Calling herself a fool, Bexlee headed to the kitchen, set up the coffee maker, and turned it on. Once she had two vats of the magical brew—both with a splash of milk—she headed to the bedroom. She placed the coffee mugs on the dresser and sat on the side of the bed.

Wynn cracked an eye open. "Do I smell coffee?"

"You do." Bexlee quirked a half smile. "Would you prefer water? Maybe both?"

The other woman glared at a glass of water sitting next to the bed. "Have water, want caffeine."

Bexlee shifted her weight to stand, but Wynn reached out and clasped her wrist. "Thank you."

"For what?" Her gut clenched at the myriad of possible answers.

"For finding me and bringing me home. I don't remember much of last night, just a lot of gin and tonic and the very pretty ocean. And the sand talking to me." Her face scrunched up. "Any idea what that was about?"

Bexlee relaxed and rubbed Wynn's forehead, pushing her hair from her face. "I don't think the beach can talk, but you did call me, then dropped your phone."

The other woman laughed. "Ow. Gods, my head. Any meds with that coffee? Why does my head still hurt?"

"You drank enough to get thoroughly drunk, an impressive feat for a wolf. Do you have anything in the house?"

"No. I never need anything for my head. My head sometimes pounds, but it fixes itself pretty quickly."

Bexlee rubbed down Wynn's back and the other woman moaned. "Okay, let's see if the coffee helps. The other cops always swear it does as much as any of their pills."

She first helped Wynn to sit up, then brought over a steaming cup of dark brew. She moved back to the dresser for her own, taking her first sip, and nearly swooning herself.

Eyes half closed and a small smile from her first sip of coffee, Wynn sighed. She looked up at Bexlee and raised an eyebrow. "Why not come back and sit with me? You don't have to hide all the way over there."

Apprehension tingled through Bexlee's body. "I didn't want to assume anything. I mean, if you don't want me here, I'll understand. I only stayed because you asked me to last night ... do you remember that?" She stayed stuck to the dresser, unsure what to do. She wanted to be supportive, but she worried about her own heart, as well. She knew she'd do almost anything for this woman, and that thought terrified her.

Wynn's face disappeared behind the vastness of the mug she drank from. Once she'd had some coffee, her body sank down, tension releasing from her shoulders. She put the mug back on the table. "Please sit with me?"

Bexlee couldn't refuse her. She walked over, placed her mug next to Wynn's and sat by the other woman's legs.

Wynn rubbed her face. "Why didn't you sleep in here ... with me?"

"You were drunk. I'm not going to sleep with you without sober consent."

"Will you come and sit next to me now? I miss your warmth—your being—next to me."

Bexlee shut her eyes and debated. She knew in the end she'd do what Wynn asked. She crawled over the other woman's legs and sat next to her, leaning on the soft headboard. Before she could stop herself, she slid an arm around Wynn's back. Wynn sighed and rested her head on Bexlee.

For a minute, Bexlee shut her eyes and pretended it was all real. They were a couple cuddling in bed together. They fit well, sitting here, sharing the moment. She soaked it in, knowing it had an endpoint.

She leaned down and kissed the top of Wynn's head.

Wynn sighed. "We need to talk."

Gods, the words of death so soon?

"Okay."

"I was brought up believing pack wolves were bullies." Bexlee stiffened at this, but Wynn continued. "When they came to a town, they eradicated all non-pack wolves. My father told me they were to be feared and avoided. When I learned about the pack here, I avoided y'all—" She shook her head and smiled. "—all of you"

"It was a different pack then." Bexlee said, rubbing Wynn's back.

Wynn looked up at Bexlee and nodded slightly. "I know. I never met the old alpha, but I saw him and his crazy friend. They came into The Silver Fox and tried to throw their weight around. The cops put them in their place."

Bexlee snorted. "I'd've loved to see that. Those two were utter asses."

"True. Tamsin did the world a big favor by taking them out. Anyway, after you, and then Tamsin, approached me, my family told me to leave. My family's belief that I'm not safe keeps being shoved down my throat. 'Leave, Wynn, find a new job in a new city. It isn't worth staying there.'"

It felt like someone punched Bexlee in the gut. "And what do you think?" Her voice was thin and soft.

Wynn's warm fingers wrapped around hers. "I think I found someone I can love. I didn't mean to do that. I didn't plan to do that, but my heart, soul, and wolf decided for me. I can't leave without dying inside."

Bexlee started trembling.

"Say something, Bexlee."

She pulled Wynn down so they lay together, bodies intertwined. "I love you, too."

Chapter 29 - Tying the Knot
Tamsin

The scents of the Sunday brunch filled the house. Tamsin knew she'd spend the week in the kitchen, but she loved spending Sundays cooking with her pack. There were three bread puddings in the oven. Jolly worked with Stewart and Rainy on deviled eggs, while Joyce and

Georgette prepared a snack board with a mountain of fruit, sausage, cheese, and bread. Paige ... well, no one wanted to end up at the hospital, so she sat at the table drinking coffee, watching.

"Will there be eggs or bacon?" Paige asked, a wispiness in her voice.

Tamsin turned and smiled. "We could have scrambled eggs and bacon. That would be easy to add to the menu."

Orin walked in from the dining room. "I've made enough coffee for an army. How much more do you think I need to make?"

"Double?" Joyce asked, working with the kids. "We can put the extra in the fridge for tomorrow. You only make your magical brew once a week; it really isn't fair."

He winked, and moved to the machine.

It didn't take long for them to move the food to the dining room. The last person to join them was Tory. Being a nurse, she worked odd hours and couldn't eat with the pack often. It was nice to see her here.

Tamsin filled her plate and turned to their resident nurse. "Tory, how goes it in the emergency room?"

She flopped down and started to fill a plate. "I'm trying to figure out what this disease is. I know it has to do with the black witches, but it's more than that. If it were only the black witches, wouldn't they only target us and the witches in town? There are a lot of vanilla humans in the morgue. That tip Wynn passed on to Bex was absolutely correct—the old woman the other day was a witch, but outside of her, only about a third have been witches. And none of the deaths have been wolves."

"Are your supervisors concerned about your interest in all of this?" Tamsin filled her own plate, pouring heated syrup over the fruit-covered bread pudding.

Tory finished off her bite, washing it down with some coffee. "I don't think anyone has noticed. With my blue hair and youthful appearance, I try to stay under the radar as much as I can." She searched the faces of the rest of the pack. "Where is Bex? I wanted to discuss a text she sent me on Friday."

"Yeah!" demanded Stewart from the kids' table. "Where is Aunt Bex? I wanna plan out Thanksgiving with her today."

"She promised us!" Rainy's face scrunched up with all her six-year-old ire.

Joyce rubbed their backs. "How about I help you two plan? I'm sure the three of us can find a lot of mischief to get into."

They grumbled, but agreed.

Before any other questions could be asked, the front door opened. As if choreographed, everyone's heads swung towards the sound.

Stewart's voice cut through the silence. "Maybe it's Aunt Bex."

Before anyone could respond, Maria and Blake entered. Joyce leapt up and gave her daughter Blake a hug. "What did you do?" she demanded.

Blake threw her head back and laughed. "I love you too, Mom."

Georgette got up and hugged Maria. "You're back! I thought you'd take more time. Did you do it?"

Maria's eyes sparkled. "We did. We didn't want to do anything like what all of you are putting Tam and Paige through."

Tamsin's heart dropped. "Holy hell, you two eloped? You really did it? And you didn't tell me?"

Maria finally laughed. "No, my humble leader. You're with Paige, and she can't keep a secret. It's the reporter in her."

Paige snorted. "Well, I never! Though, you aren't wrong. Congratulations, my friends. That's amazing."

"No, it isn't!" Joyce demanded. "I wasn't invited to my daughter's wedding, my *only* daughter's wedding."

Blake smiled at her sheepishly. "We'll have a big celebration in two months. January needs something big anyway. I'll even let you plan it, Mom. Deal?"

Joyce glared. "Fine, but you'll do whatever I say."

Blake tried to blank her face and to mollify her mother, but she kept snorting. "Yes, Mom."

Chapter 30 - A Little Bit of Science
Bexlee

Monday morning, Bexlee woke up, body entwined with Wynn. They'd spent Sunday together talking and cuddling. It had been everything she'd hoped for. Now she needed to get home, change for work, and get to work, all before the sun rose.

She pushed herself up, then gave Wynn a quick kiss, careful not to wake her. Bexlee had put her clothes in the guest bathroom the day before. After she ran through the shower and got dressed, she found a travel mug of coffee by the door with a note.

Bexlee. Thanks again for a magical weekend. I'll text when I'm up. I'm apprehensive about dinner with the pack tonight, but I promised I'd do it, and I will. Love you, Wynn.

Emotions tingled in her chest, and she tucked the note in her back pocket. The drive to pack house was quick without any cars on the road.

After she changed, she found Tamsin in the kitchen. "What are you doing up this early?"

"You weren't here yesterday, and I knew this would be the only time I'd see you if I wanted to speak with you. I take it things are better with you and the loan officer?"

Bexlee couldn't stop the smile that popped up on her face, or the heat blossoming on her cheeks. "She said she'd come for dinner tonight, meet the pack."

Tamsin's brows crept up. "Really? When I met her she seemed very opposed to that."

"Yeah, she was brought up to hate any pack wolf. I think she sees us differently now. I'm both excited and terrified about what will happen when she meets everyone, but I love her, Tam ... she has to meet my family."

Tamsin pulled her into a hug and kissed the top of her head. "Good. Go to work and I'll get things arranged here."

A weight lifted from Bexlee's shoulders. "Thanks. I'll be home early today ... I hope."

She grabbed a protein bar and a banana, and headed to the precinct. Once there, she lost herself in the stacks of reports and files on her desk.

Midmorning, Cyrus called a meeting to discuss their current case. He stood in front of a group of cops. "The labs have found a chemical in several of the heart attack victims. We need to look at local scientists. See if we can find a link to our deceased or suspects, especially Wynn Taylor, who recently has been our prime suspect. That said, we should broaden our search to anyone working at Brian Simms Mortgage Lenders."

The cop across from Bexlee lifted a finger, but spoke without waiting. "Are we looking at the bigger companies, or private firms?"

"Anyone and everyone. We're not sure who is doing this, but there is a common thread."

The chief leaned back. "Can our people identify the drug? Do we know what's doing this?"

Cyrus's face flattened and he shook his head. "No, sir, they're completely at a loss. They can find traces of the same compound proving there is something linking these people, but they can't figure out what it is. They've called in other experts. If we can figure out the ingredients, that could help track who's creating this drug."

Bexlee massaged her temples. *Magic, that's what they're missing. It has to be a concoction that needs magic to activate it. That's the only thing that makes sense. It's more than just ingredients.*

"Can the lab tell if the drug acts instantly?" Bexlee wasn't sure how much the human scientists could tell from their mass spectroscopy and microscopes.

"It's pretty fast acting." Cyrus grabbed some papers and flipped through them. "They predict anywhere from one to three days in the system. Though possibly faster depending on if it's in a liquid or solid state. Some of this is guess work since some people, like that woman from the car, died while driving."

Another officer looked up from taking notes. "So, we're looking for scientists connected to these people. They are probably local, so, don't start outside of the greater Santa Cruz area? Should we look at professors at the college?"

"Look at anyone with the science to do the thing."

The chief slapped his hands on the table. "Okay, people, you know what you need to do. If you have more questions, see Officer Ezra. Otherwise, let's find this man."

Bexlee rolled her eyes. "Or woman?"

The chief froze, then laughed. "Or woman. Get to it, people, we have a case to solve, and I personally would like this done before Thanksgiving."

Chapter 31 - Entering Enemy Territory
Wynn

The first day back at work was so much worse than Wynn had imagined. She had one appointment with a client, and that hour was an amazing relief in an ocean of emotional hell. During the morning meeting, Brian tried to be sensitive, but the reality of needing to hire new loan officers was pressing on him. Though Wynn knew it was important, it hurt her soul to hear the discussion or replacing her friends so soon after they'd been murdered.

Once the meeting ended, she headed to the break room for some of her sweet tea. Silas followed her. "Can I have some of that?"

"Really? You've never wanted any before."

He shrugged. "I just need something sweet after the sourness of that meeting."

She snorted. "Facts. Yeah, grab two glasses. I have enough to share."

Sophia walked in. "Make that three. You know I'm addicted to that stuff."

Back in her office, Wynn prepped for the next few weeks. She had clients coming in every day, morning and afternoon. She pulled bank records and credit scores and spent time watching the market. She felt the percentage for locking loans would go down after Thanksgiving.

By the end of the day, she regretted agreeing to have dinner with the pack. *Am I ready to enter enemy territory and break bread with them?*

She texted Bexlee. Are you home? I don't want to face the wolves without you.

The text bubbles danced for a while. `I'm leaving now. I need to shower. Unless you want to shower with me, give me forty-five minutes and I can meet you at the door.`

Warmth bubbled in her. `Is the shower a real offer?`

A laugh emoji popped up quickly. Wynn put the phone in her pocket and walked to her car. She decided to head to The Zesty Bean and get a pastry. Before she got her car started, her phone vibrated. `The offer is always real, but the house is full of wolves with great hearing.`

A growl slipped out. *Damn pack!* `Want something from The Zesty Bean?`

The trip to the café through traffic frustrated her, but being there was an island of calm in her day. She knew dinner wouldn't be any better than her day at work.

While waiting in line, she received a text from Bexlee. `Home now, about to get in the shower, chocolate croissant please.`

Wynn had arrived at the counter and put in her order: two croissants and a small coffee. While she waited she texted back: `Naked and about to` shower, and no picture? You are a tease!

"Flynn!"

She rolled her eyes at the messed up name, and collected her things. At the table she saw Bexlee had replied. There was a picture of her naked leg from the knee down. This is my first naked text, how am I doing?

Wynn laughed out loud, disrupting the man sitting at the table next to her and typing on his computer. Nailed it!

Finishing her coffee, Wynn collected the bag with the two pastries, and headed off to pack house. She'd taken a page out of Bexlee's playbook and packed an overnight bag just in case. She couldn't actually imagine sleeping in this vipers' den. She hoped to convince Bexlee to come home with her.

After she knocked, Bexlee greeted her with a hug and a quick kiss. "I'm so glad you're here. Thank you for coming."

"If it's awful, I'll just have to punish you later."

Bexlee's laugh was a bit high pitched. "Just remember, none of our conversations are private ... and my dads can hear you."

Wynn patted her cheek, then pulled her in for a kiss. "You're so cute when you're nervous."

The entrance led to a large living room. There were people scattered all over the room, including two girls. Squinting, Wynn realized one of the young girls was a boy in a dress. She smiled. *Maybe these people aren't so bad.*

Bexlee twined her fingers with Wynn's. "Dylan, Easton, this is Wynn. Wynn, these are my dad's."

Before either of the men sitting on the loveseat could say anything, the boy jumped up. "And I'm Stewart, her nephew, but you can call me Stew if you're a friend. Do you like this dress? It's blue."

Wynn turned and looked down at the boy. "It *is* blue, and pretty ... or handsome."

"I am handsome. I'm a handsome boy. I like wearing dresses, 'cause they're comfortable, and easier to move in."

"They are."

His face got serious as he seemed to gauge if she truly agreed, then he sat back down to play with a box of Legos.

"Right," Bexlee mumbled. "We're going to go into the kitchen, now."

Bexlee dragged her through a door on the far side of the room. A room that would fit half her house with two stoves, four ovens, a double-wide refrigerator, and a massive expanse of counter spaces stood before her.

"Don't drool, Wynn, it's just a kitchen."

Her jaw dropped. "Just a kitchen? *Just* a kitchen? Do you hear the words that are coming out of your mouth?"

A smaller round table sat in a windowed alcove. Kids' projects covered it.

Someone chuckled from her right. There was a farm table that would fit twelve easily. In a side chair sat a Latinx woman. Bexlee continued to pull Wynn in her direction. They took seats across from her. "Hi, Georgette, this is Wynn. Wynn, this is Georgette. She was one of my babysitters when I was growing up."

Georgette smiled at them. "It's nice to finally meet you. Welcome to the looney bin."

A man and woman walked in.

"I can't believe you haven't started cooking yet," the man said.

"Orin, it's tacos. How long do you think it'll take?"

Bexlee perked up. "Connie, you're making dinner tonight? You're not at the restaurant?"

The woman looked at Bexlee and her face softened. "Tam woke me up this morning and asked for a favor. I called the restaurant. They can survive without me for a night. Not to mention, Mondays are never that busy."

Wynn watched, confused. "She cooks?"

Dancing in her seat, Bexlee nodded. "She's the head chef at Ocean Sunrise. She usually only cooks on full moon run nights. This is going to be fantastic."

When Wynn first got to Santa Cruz, her firm had a staff meeting at Ocean Sunrise. The meal had been over the top spectacular. And *that* chef was standing here, in the pack house, about to cook tacos? She repressed the urge to drool.

A man walked in who looked a bit like Bexlee. Same blue eyes and blond hair. He was muscular and wore a t-shirt with a firefighter emblem on the pocket. "Bex, Stew said you had a friend?"

Bexlee smirked and shook her head. "Toby, this is Wynn, my friend. Wynn, this lunker is my brother, Toby."

He sat down across from Wynn. "So, what do you do to take up your time?"

"Mostly drink sweet tea and play the market."

He laughed. "About time Bex found someone sassy and smart."

The sizzle of meat came from the stove and the smell of seasoning filled the air. Wynn leaned forward. *Time to cause trouble!* "Tell me stories."

Next to her, she saw Bexlee glare at her brother. "Think hard, Toby, about your next words."

Toby waved her off. "When Bex was eight, Maria and Georgette convinced her she was going to be entered into a dance competition."

"For fuck's sake." Bexlee mumbled next to her.

Down the table, Georgette snickered.

"So, Bexlee had never taken any dance lessons, so she started watching dance routines online. She practiced in her room for hours."

An image of a tiny Bexlee twirling around a small and very pink bedroom, knocking down a lamp surrounded by Legos, flitted through Wynn's head. She tried not to laugh. Bexlee had put her head down, mumbling about killing her brother later. Trying to calm her down, Wynn rubbed her back.

Orin brought a tray of shot glasses over and a bottle of tequila. He winked at Georgette's narrowed eyes. "What? Tacos. It's on theme. I'll make margaritas, too. But, Bex needs this if Toby is in a mood."

Toby started pouring double shots. "So, she figured out different aspects of her application routine. She'd come and show us what she'd learned. Well, she'd show Georgette and Maria. I was sometimes there, but I was only ten, I really didn't care."

"So, what happened?" Wynn was completely invested in young Bexlee's dream.

A couple walked in; one could be Georgette's sister, the other a tall, blonde knock-out. The one who could be Georgette's sister smiled at them. "Bexlee added a cartwheel and spin. She ended up breaking her leg during practice. Only her shift to werewolf and fast healing kept her out of the hospital. Me and Georgette got into a heap of trouble, though."

A male's voice echoed from the living room. "I still don't think this story is funny and it's been almost twenty years."

Toby rolled his eyes. "Aw, Dad. Come on!"

Bexlee finally lifted her head and threw back two shots of tequila. "Wynn, meet Maria and Blake. They just eloped, much to Blake's mom's chagrin." She said the last in a mock whisper.

Wynn grabbed her own shot of tequila. "A movie would be less amusing than you lot, you know that, right?"

By the time the food arrived, they'd each had a few more shots, and started in on the margaritas. Wynn didn't think she'd remember all the names of the people she'd met, but she enjoyed the evening more than she'd predicted.

The food was good, but not enough to justify the chance of driving home after all the drinks. The overnight bag was a must.

Chapter 32 - Catching a Suspect
Bexlee

A warm mouth on hers. Bexlee moaned as she shifted. A weight rolled onto her. A tongue slipped into her mouth and a hand settled on her breast. She pushed into the hand as warmth built in her.

Bexlee woke up to Wynn's hazel eyes. Wynn's hand smoothed down Bexlee's stomach to her clit. Bexlee reached up, stroking Wynn side to her breast, as their mouths continued to explore.

With electricity of pleasure pulsing through her body, Bexlee flipped them so she could straddle Wynn. The other woman's hand was still rubbing and playing with her sex. She leaned down to press a line of kisses along Wynn's neck to her ear, sucking in the lobe, scraping it out between her lips.

Wynn's groan vibrated in her ear.

As Bexlee licked around the edge of Wynn's ear and kissed down her neck, Wynn thrust fingers inside Bexlee, finding a rhythm that had her moaning with every breath.

At the juncture of Wynn's neck and shoulder, Bexlee bit down, dragging her teeth over the silky skin, then kissing the spot. Wynn's head rolled to the side, giving her more access. Bexlee's body rolled with the motion of Wynn's hand as she nibbled down towards her perfect breasts.

At her target, she sucked in a nipple, her hand traveling down Wynn's body to reciprocate.

Wynn's free hand clasped Bexlee's chin and pulled her back up to a deep kiss. Her tongue demanded entrance into her mouth. Her hand was making the world fracture, and Bexlee cried out into Wynn's mouth.

A moment later, Wynn screamed out Bexlee's name.

Bexlee collapsed on the other woman, breathing hard. Once she could think ... and speak, she said, "Morning, love. Is this the plan for waking up?"

Wynn laughed. "Maybe. It seems like a good way to wake up to me."

"True, but now I want to stay here with you, but I have to go to work."

"Thursday night you'll come to my house, and Friday we'll sleep in."

Bexlee growled. "I have to work Friday, but not Saturday."

"Gods alive, am I really falling for a police officer?"

Bexlee attacked her and gave her a deep kiss. "Yes, yes, you are."

She got out of bed, found work clothes, and got dressed. Wynn put on clothes with her. The house was quiet, the two of them up much earlier than the rest of the pack. They headed to The Zesty Bean for coffee and a breakfast sandwich. Once they had their order, Wynn asked, "Is the kitchen closed this early? Is there a reason you don't just make coffee and something in that grand room the pack house has?"

"Um, no. I'm just not that much of a kitchen person."

"So, I could've used that glorious room this morning? Made coffee and anything I wanted, and no one would've minded?"

"Of course, not. Any time you want."

Wynn snarled. "Next time, Bexlee, next time. To the moon!"

Bexlee laughed. "Okay, I get it."

They finished their breakfast, and Bexlee headed to work. She was working on a list of scientists. They needed to find a suspect.

Just after nine, something about one of the people she researched clicked. "Cyrus, come look at this. It seems too perfect. Like, how did we miss it? I think my brain is melting and I'm seeing things."

Cyrus came to stand over her shoulder. He read the computer screen. Then he pushed her chair and started typing on her keyboard. Screens flew on the monitor. "Chief!" he bellowed. "Court found a suspect. Send two cars. I've emailed you the files."

The whole room erupted in voices and activity. There was still work, and the search for potential suspects wasn't over. The person Bexlee found wasn't a guaranteed hit, but he fit their profile perfectly.

It wasn't until after lunch that the man was brought in. Loui Vala, looking like a model with ash-brown curls and facial hair that framed his face. His blue eyes cased the room, landing on her with a smirk. He tried to stop walking, but the officers dragged him to an interview room.

Cyrus leaned across his desk towards her. "Do you know him?"

"No, I don't."

"Good, then let's go. It's interview time."

As she walked towards the room, she felt her phone vibrate. A text from Wynn. She'd reply right after the interview.

Chapter 33 - Work Time Drama
Wynn

"So, if you wait to lock in your rate until December, my guess is, you'll get a better deal. There's no guarantee, but the rates seem a bit high right now."

The couple watched her like doe-eyed infants. The wife just nodded, while the husband's eyes narrowed. "How certain are you about the rate lowering?"

"There's no guarantee, but the trend in the market is heading that way. It's higher right now than it's been all quarter." Wynn pointed at a few charts she'd printed out to make the information easier for her clients to understand.

The man's face hardened. "So, it could continue to go up. We should lock in right now before it gets worse."

Wynn took a deep, cleansing breath. "Well, that's one way to look at it, but with how high it is now, that isn't likely."

He glanced down at her chest then up at her face. "And you said Silas was too busy to work with us?"

"Yes, he's booked for the rest of this week and next. If you want to move forward on buying your house, then you'll need to work with me."

His upper lip twitched. "I'd like to lock in the rate today, before it skyrockets." He gazed at his wife. "Right dear?"

Wide eyed, she merely nodded. Wynn didn't think she'd heard a word from her since she'd introduced herself after entering her office.

Wynn kept her face tightly controlled as she finished their paperwork. "Very well."

As they left her office, she heard them running into Silas in the hall.

"That *woman* you work with tried to convince us to wait on locking in a rate, can you believe it? The trends are going up, and she wanted us to wait!" the man almost yelled, accusatory.

Wynn dropped her head into her hand as it began to pound. Maybe she could get some sweet tea when the hallway cleared out. *Gods, I miss Meghan. She'd slay that couple. The audacity of them.*

"I hope you did. The rates are awful right now. Wynn has her finger on the pulse of the market better than anyone I know. It's why I entrusted you to her. You took her advice, didn't you?" He barely gave the man time to think, much less answer. Wynn heard a pounding, which she assumed was a slap on the back. "Of course, you did. What else would you do?"

The voices receded towards the front of the office. Wynn could've listened in, but she was ready to be done for the day. It was barely past noon, and all she wanted to do was head home.

When she was about ready to head to the break room for her sweet tea, Silas came into her office and fell into one of her client chairs. "Can we talk?"

Straightening, she thought of a million reasons she didn't want to talk to him, but he had just stood up for her. "Sure. What's up?"

"You have a friend on the police force, right?"

The fuck?

She tried to keep her voice neutral. "What's wrong, Silas?"

His whole body crumpled in the chair. "It's Loui; he was arrested. He doesn't know why. He had one phone call and, well, he didn't call me, but someone at his work called me saying he was arrested."

"Wait. He didn't call you? I thought you two were really close. Who would he have called?" Wynn's mind whirled with the news.

"I don't know!" Silas wailed. "But you know a cop, right? Can you find out why he was arrested? It has to be a misunderstanding. Loui is a pussy cat. He wouldn't hurt a fly."

"Yes, of course. Why don't you go back to your office, and I'll let you know when I know anything."

He just sat in the chair, frozen.

With a sigh, she took out her phone. Hey, do you know anything about the arrest of a guy named Loui– "What's his last name?"

Silas licked his lips. "Vala, Loui Vala."

212

"Right, okay." -Vala? Apparently he's a friend of someone I work with and he's worried. No rush, he's just worried.

There was no immediate response, or even any indication Bexlee got the message. "I'm sorry; my friend must be off doing something. Really, I'll let you know when I get any response."

Finally, Silas nodded and left.

Wynn hoped Bexlee replied having no idea who Loui was. There were plenty of precincts in town. What was the likelihood Bexlee knew anything about the situation?

Chapter 34 - And Another One Bites the Dust
Bexlee

"Once again, I don't know Josh Wilde or his wife Tonya Wilde. I've told you that already, three times. I never met Meghan Lee or Korah Zinus. I get that they worked with Silas, but he and I haven't been a couple that long, so I don't know why you think I'd know the people he works with. I'm sorry these people have died, but, for the umpteenth time, you're looking at the wrong person."

He lied. Every time they asked him these questions, he lied. Bexlee couldn't explain to Cyrus why she knew he lied—that she was a werewolf, and therefore could smell a lie—but she knew. It was both the best and worst part of her job.

"We have evidence of you and Mr. James— Silas—taking Korah Zinus out dancing two weeks ago." She found a picture in a manila folder she'd downloaded from Korah's phone. She slid it across the desk. "Should we start at the beginning?"

His face flat, he dropped his dead eyes to the pictures, emotionless. "Ah. Korah. That's right. I guess I have met the girl. She was such a soggy noodle, I guess I forgot. Do you have more photos in there to catch me in compromising pictures with Mr. and Mrs. Wilde? And what's her name— Meghan?"

Cyrus's face hardened. "This would all go much smoother, Mr. Vala, if you'd just tell us the truth. I believe we'd all like to get out of here today. How about this—my partner and I will give you a half hour to think about these people. We'll even leave the images to help jog your memory. Then we'll come back and review our questions."

He practically snarled, "Fine. But I'll want a lawyer for the next round of questions." He pulled out a card. "Call him." He slammed the card down. Cyrus picked the card up, and the two of them walked out.

When the click of the door sounded, Bexlee squeezed her eyes shut. "For the love of all that is mighty, he is a pill and a half."

"Go, get some fresh air; I'll call the lawyer."

"I'm going to get coffee down the street. Want some?"

Cyrus's eyes twinkled. "And a scone?"

"Fine, and a scone."

"You know, this would be easier if my first conclusion that there were witches, and it was all a big magic trick were true."

Bexlee grabbed her purse. "I don't know if it'd be easier, but then all we'd have to do is stop the magic. Is that what you'd want to be, a magic-user? Do you play D&D?"

He looked down at himself. "Naw, but I know about it, my nephew plays. Anyway, I'd want to be a werebear. Look how big and hairy I am. Wouldn't that be cool? Werebear ... There bear!" He fell into his chair laughing.

Shaking her head, Bexlee headed out to get coffee. On the way, she read Wynn's text. Her stomach fell when she read it. She texted back. Need-to-know. Big bad. Talk more tonight?

After she'd ordered in the café, Wynn's response came. Since I'd hoped you didn't know what was going on, I'm going to tell Silas you don't know. Wrong precinct. You don't have to tell me, but you can. I'm safe ... good with secrets.

A buzz of warm fuzzies attacked Bexlee's insides as she collected the coffee and pastries. She'd gotten three coffees—one for the chief—and a box of scones. There had been a bevy of people working on the case today. Everyone deserved a bit of something sweet.

She brought everything into the conference room. Drinking coffee and eating scones, they discussed more connections with Loui and the dead bodies.

"Can we connect him with Meghan yet?"

"No, Chief. Not her or the clients."

"We can connect him to the kid from the college last month. They attended the same LGBTQ+ group at the UU church."

All in all, they found five more connections. It was enough. Cyrus and Bexlee felt fortified enough to go face the man.

Another officer ran into the conference room. "Chief! Chief! Come quick! The suspect ... he's dead!"

Chapter 35 - Giving Thanks
Tamsin

The kitchen was full to bursting. Tamsin would normally be helping—she loved to cook—but today she had too much to be thankful for, and wanted to spend time thinking about the last few months.

She leaned on the door frame, watching the cook prepare a meal that would feed seventeen wolves and a few others. Her head felt like it would explode thinking about that number. Seventeen. Back in March when she had arrived after hearing of her aunt's death, the pack had four—maybe five—people, depending on if you included Paige.

Connie stood at the counter, slicing and dicing. Maria was making rolls. Tamsin blinked; Wynn worked at a station with potatoes and Brussels sprouts. Blake and Bexlee sat at the table, the assigned 'go-to' runners for the day. Joyce sat at the table with Rainy and Stewart.

In the living room, tables had been set up. A group played Settlers of Catan, another group played cards. Tamsin walked down the hall and out to the back yard, where Jolly and Timothy sat drinking wine. Jolly smiled up at her. "Come to join the only two sane people in the pack?"

"Really? You think you're the ones with reason?"

Jolly lifted her glass. "We're out here, drinking wine—away from the cooking and any squabbling from games. Tell me, Tam, where have we gone wrong?"

She laughed. "Fair enough. But, no, I'm just checking in on everyone. I want to make sure everyone is relaxing, doing what they want. It's good to see you two found your thing."

"We sure have. And if you weren't alpha, what would you be doing?"

"I'd probably still be alone in Chicago, and that would suck. But, to answer your real question, I'd be one of the insane ones cooking. You know that. But this year I want to just take it all in."

Timothy looked behind her. "Where's Paige?"

"Winning money at the card table. She's a shark."

He snorted. "Good to know. I'll avoid the card table when she's there."

Tamsin headed back in, and Paige met her in the hallway. She wrapped her in a hug. "Hi, love."

"Hey, I thought you were playing cards."

"I missed you. I wanted to ask you what you were thankful for before we sat with an army of hungry wolves."

"Umhmm, you were kicked out of the game?"

"No! Well, yes. But that's because Toby is a sore loser."

Tamsin laughed and pulled her in for a kiss.

There are so many people. The dining room table normally seated sixteen, but could fit twenty-four. They had twenty for dinner, and with all the food, they had it fully extended. Even the kids were at the table with them. Everyone waited for the food to be served before chatting with the people seated near them. The cacophony of voices filled the room.

Tamsin turned to Bexlee. "Tell me again about this suspect. I'm guessing Tory would like to hear this."

Bexlee looked down the table, but most of the pack was involved with their own conversations. "We don't know what happened. Well, *officially* we don't know what happened. I have a theory, but I can't put it in any report. It's the hardest part of my job."

"Tell me about it," Tory groused. "Let me guess, he's a witch, and they sent the curse his way to shut him up."

Bexlee nodded. "Yeah, as soon as he died, the witch scent flooded the room. All I can guess is he was a black witch. They must be the ones doing this. They have a way to hide their scent from us."

Tory was nodding. "I agree. Not all the deceased have the chemical in their system. It's mostly just the humans."

Wynn's face twisted. "I get that he was Silas's boy toy, but why target all his work people? Do you think he knew I was a wolf, and it was about me or am I being self-centered?"

Bexlee wrapped an arm around her. "We may never know. If only he hadn't ended up dead before we'd gotten any real answers from him." She turned to Tamsin. "Hey, Tam, are any of the witches necromancers?"

Wynn's eyes grew to saucers. "Wait, is that a thing?"

Tory laughed. "I wish. That would be excellent."

Paige gave her an odd look. "Thanks for giving me new nightmares, Tory." She shifted her gaze to Wynn. "Every day I learn about new oddities in this world. I'm glad to know that zombies won't be one of them. Unless, of course, Tory has her way."

Tory laughed. "I mean, none of my supervisors notice what I'm doing. I probably could try to figure it out."

From down the table Georgette's voice rang out. "No, Tory—no zombies!"

The backyard was a madhouse! Sixteen werewolves! Thank goodness; Katt, a witch connected to one of the wolves, decided to join them for the day. She said she'd watch over Stewart and Rainy while they ran. It wasn't a full moon night so the run wasn't necessary, just tradition. A night they all had off. A night they could run and be free.

Tamsin asked that they become furry in shifts. She and Paige were in the last group, along with Bexlee, Wynn, and Tory. Everyone else had slipped out to the woods.

The shift, as always, was quick, but painful. The body doing what no body was meant to do— bones cracking and reshaping, hair receding and growing in new places. Fingers and toes becoming paws and claws.

Searching the wolves around her, she saw Bexlee's gray wolf with her blue eyes shining, ready to run. Tory's black wolf, a demon with her bouncing exuberance. Paige stood next to Tory, her photo opposite, white as a cloud, save for a few dark markings. The only wolf new to Tamsin was Wynn. She matched Bexlee, a bit larger, but a beautiful gray, with intense hazel eyes.

Tamsin howled, and the five of them ran out to meet the others.

Chapter 36 - Black Friday!
Bexlee

The low buzzing of the phone woke Bexlee up. She found her phone and turned it off, hoping it didn't wake up Wynn. Their bodies were entwined, and she wanted to stay that way for the day, but she was lucky to get

Thanksgiving off. She wasn't getting Friday off as well.

Wynn's back was to her, her own sleeping teddy bear. Kissing Wynn's shoulder, she gave the woman a squeeze, then gently separated herself.

The night before, Wynn had set up an overnight oatmeal breakfast jar. She said it would be easy enough even for her. Bexlee had been offended, but also thought Wynn overstated her abilities, especially before five a.m.

She pressed the button to turn on the coffee maker and started on the oatmeal. By the time the coffee was done, she'd finished her food. She poured the coffee in the travel mug, and was proud of her ingenuity so early in the morning. Finding a pad of paper, she left Wynn a note. *Thanks for breakfast and coffee. Love you. B.*

In the office, she found a chocolate croissant on her desk. Cyrus came to sit next to her. "Morning, Court, hope you had a good day off. Those of us working had a long day."

"Anything interesting happen?"

"No, thankfully. Maybe today will be equally slow, and then it'll be the weekend."

She smiled at him. "Do you have any plans for the weekend?"

"I'm going to sit by my fire pit and drink beer."

"Sounds nice. Have someone to share that with?"

His head fell back. "Nope. Just me, myself, and I. Why, want to bring that loan officer of yours over and hang out with your partner on your time off?"

"Sure, maybe. Let me ask Wynn, but sounds good to me."

Cyrus sat up. "Really?"

"Why not? Why does this surprise you?"

"It's just—"

"Ezra! Court! My office, now!" The chief's voice rang out, filling the room.

They stood. Bexlee grabbed a pad and pen from her desk and followed Cyrus into the chief's office. She shut the door before sitting down.

"Another body's been found in that nature preserve area by the college. I want you to go out and follow up with the other cops out there. Find out if it's another heart attack. I thought we'd figured this out."

They stood and headed out. Cyrus drove. "What do you think it is?"

"I don't know. A cluster fuck?"

He laughed. "The scientists said it could take up to three or four days. I mean, we nabbed the guy on Tuesday. If the person was hit on Tuesday, they could've died Wednesday or Thursday, and weren't found until today."

"We're also not thinking about how the drug was administered or ingested. If it's in food, how long is it stable and lethal? The attack could've been put in place weeks ago and only just now eaten or drunk. Too many questions."

Cyrus rubbed his head with his free hand. "Well, fuck. And the report on that suspect's toxicity comes in today. Not everyone had the concoction in their system."

"Maybe we're back to your theory of magic, my friend."

Cyrus laughed as he parked in the arboretum parking lot.

They headed out to where the report stated the body was found, and the voices Bexlee could hear. As she got closer, she could smell the death of the person. When they finally arrived, she could also smell the herby scent that marked this woman—witch.

She squatted down to get a better look at the woman. She had brown hair, tangled in knots around her head. Her skirt and shirt were skewed. "She looks dumped here, like the others. Was there any identification?"

One of the other cops held a purse. "Name's Elena Thompson. She doesn't live far. Wallet filled with cash, so robbery's not the motive. No cell phone though."

Desperate to get answers, Bexlee shut her eyes and focused on Tamsin. She rarely reached out to her alpha mentally, but it *was* an option. The connection was stronger when they were wolves. *"Tamsin, it's Bexlee. Can I ask you a question?"*

The answer came quickly. *"Of course. I avoid black Friday shopping. I'm lazing around the house today. What's up?"*

Bexlee wanted to take a deep breath, but the air stank of death and witch. *"Is Elena Thompson one of Cinthia's coven?"*

Somehow the connection got sharper. It was almost as if Tamsin lasered in on Bexlee. *"Yes, why?"*

"I'm out in the woods behind the school. She's the latest victim."

Bexlee stood and began gathering other evidence. She couldn't stay squatted too long and not get weird attention. Cyrus spoke with the lead cop from the other precinct, she heard him say his name was Officer Summers. She'd have to check into him. His report was solid-sounding.

When Tamsin reconnected with her, she'd found a trail that looked promising,. *"Cinthia knows. She's coming to meet me for coffee and a tour of the campus. We'll take a hike and happen on by there. Maybe in an hour?"*

"That works. Sorry about the bad news."

Bexlee got back to work, wishing she could've taken two days off.

Chapter 37 - Yes Ma'am, Can I Have Another?
Wynn

The bed was cold when Wynn woke up. She wondered if it was worth waking up at the ass crack of dawn to see Bexlee off to work. She doubted it. In the end, she did love her sleep. She stretched and thought about what she'd do.

I could brave the crowds for a sale on something I don't need. She chuckled as she slipped from bed and headed to the bathroom.

Once done with that, she found Bexlee had reset the coffee maker for her, cleaned the pot, and put new coffee grounds in the top. In the fridge, there was a glass containing the extra coffee from her pot.

Hmm. Options. Hot coffee or iced coffee?

Deciding she wanted to start the day with something warm, she turned on the machine and found the note. She smiled, then started making herself some eggs and toast.

Her phone rang. "Hi, Dad, what do you want?"

"Happy Thanksgiving, darlin'. You didn't call yesterday. I worried that pack found you and did you in. You always call on Thanksgiving."

She sighed. *Always judging me about something.* "Did you and the gang have fun? Big meal, big run?"

"You know we did. How about you? You usually go to that woman's house, but you said she died. Did you spend the evening alone? Did you get out for a run?"

Wynn thought about following Tamsin's large red wolf, and running with a horde of other wolves.

It had been exhilarating. She never knew a run could feel like that.

As they had run through the woods, branches scratching their backs, birds taking off in fear at the howls of the others, Wynn felt more connected to Bexlee, like she was part of her, an extension of her body.

The pack had run out far, and found a black-tailed deer. Together, they'd taken it down. By the time they'd returned, she knew she never wanted to run alone again. The magic that made them one, made her part of them, gave her a sense of home and belonging. She'd never felt that during runs with her family, but they didn't have an alpha. They were a bunch of lone wolves.

By the end, she'd decided she'd speak with Tamsin about joining the pack. It was time she became part of something. As she'd thought the words, a warmth had flooded her, and she'd heard Tamsin's voice in her head. *"Welcome!"*

She smiled at the memory. "I did. I ate a big meal. I ran. It was good. Don't worry about me, Dad. Everything here in Santa Cruz is fine." She wasn't sure how she'd tell him she'd gone to the dark side. But she knew the conversation had to be in person. She wasn't sure their relationship would survive that revelation, but she'd cross that bridge when she got there. She had Bexlee and knew she didn't have to go it alone.

"If you're sure, darlin'. When are we gonna see you again?"

She smiled. She missed her family, as much as they pissed her off. "Soon, I promise. I'll figure out a time I can get away and visit. With all the upheaval at work, I don't know that they'll be able to have any of us leave for some time."

"Yeah, I can see that. Well, I'll talk to you soon. Don't go shopping today without a knife, y'hear?"

She laughed and hung up.

A bath. I am going to take a long bath with a good book.

Once done, she saw she had a text from Bexlee. They'd both been invited to her partner's place to hang out the next day. She decided she wanted to bring some homemade sweet tea to share, but she'd left her extra jug at work for next week. She was too lazy from her bath to make more. That was a chore for Sunday. They could stop by work on the way and pick it up.

Chapter 38 - Not as Sweet as You Think
Bexlee

"Wait, we have to stop at my work for a jug of my sweet tea."

Bexlee stood outside her car and gaped at Wynn. She looked amazing in her painted-on jeans and loose, emerald green blouse. Bexlee had wanted to strip them off her as soon as she'd put them on. Then again, the woman would look hot in a potato sack.

She shook her head. "We need to do what?" She finally managed to get the car door open.

Wynn had already slid into the car and was securing her belt. "Well, do you have something to bring? And my tea is fantastic, admit it."

"Absolutely, but isn't there some here?"

"Only half a jug. That's tacky. We need to bring a full jug, and I have *that* at work."

Squeezing her eyes shut as she closed the door and reached for her own belt, Bexlee nodded in understanding. "Okay, go to Brian Simmons, then to Cyrus's place. It isn't too far out of the way. Then a day of rest and relaxation. Got it."

Wynn leaned over for a kiss. Bexlee was more than willing to oblige.

The traffic was light. Most people had gotten their shopping done yesterday and wanted to go in for one more day of family celebrations before heading back to the real world.

"Are you ready for the beginning of holiday cheer ... like, everywhere?"

Bexlee looked at decorations going up all around, lights and trees. "I guess."

"Do you want to help me decorate my house?"

"Yes?"

Wynn laughed. "You don't have to. I love this time of year. Don't worry, you brought *me* to the dark side of pack life, I'll bring *you* to the dark side of Christmas. Before you know it, you'll be singing Christmas songs in November."

A shiver ran down Bexlee's spine. "Heaven forbid!"

They got to Wynn's office and she grabbed the tea, then they were off to Cyrus's house. He lived in a small one-bedroom home a few blocks from the beach. It looked weather-beaten, but well loved. Bexlee parked.

Before they could knock, Cyrus opened up and greeted them with his big smile. "Welcome! Ms. Taylor, it is nice to see you smiling."

"Wynn, please. Let's end the formality and leave all that unpleasantness behind us."

He enfolded her in a hug. "Perfect." He pulled back. "Come in, come in. Right on through to the back. I'll take this—what is it?"

Wynn winked at him. "Only the best sweet tea this side of the Mississippi. I thought I'd share."

"Excellent. I'll bring some glasses out. We'll start with these. There are some appetizers out there."

There was a table set up next to an outdoor kitchen. On the table were a selection of foods, including jalapeño poppers, crackers with different toppings, hummus with dippers, hamburger sliders, and a variety of chips. Bexlee's stomach growled in approval.

"How many were you planning on feeding?"

He stepped up behind her, placing down a tray with the tea and glasses. "I've seen you eat, my friend. I'm sure you'll put a pretty dent in this spread. Now, let's enjoy the good weather."

They all filled a plate and took a glass of tea. There were other harder drinks available as well. Wynn mixed them each her favorite drink, and they sat to trade stories.

Bexlee followed Cyrus to fill her second plate when he started to shake his left arm. "What did you put in that drink of yours, Wynn? I'm starting to feel all tingly."

Wynn's gaze snapped to him. "It was just your average sweet tea. Nothing to make you feel weird."

"Are you sure?" Cyrus began to sway, and Bexlee darted over to him. "I'm feeling—" He crashed down. Bexlee barely had time to pillow his head before it hit the ground.

Wynn jumped up and smelled the sweet tea. "Fuck! There's something in here. I didn't think to smell it, but it isn't my recipe. It doesn't taste different, but it smells different. I'm guessing someone put something in it. What should we do?"

Bexlee's mind raced. *Cyrus can't die. He's too good of a man, too good of a cop. And ... gods above, he's my friend.*

She looked at Wynn desperately. "He can't die."

Wynn shook her head. "I'll call 911."

"No, wait. Let me do something first."

Bexlee closed her eyes. *"Tamsin. Help, he's dying. It was in the sweet tea. He can't die!"*

"Slow down, Bex. I don't know what you're talking about."

In as few words as she could, she explained the situation. She tried to add images, but her mind was a jumble.

Care and love came from her alpha. *"This is tricky, Bex. Do you trust him?"*

"With my life. Every day, forever."

"But would he want this? Changing a person who doesn't want this is a horrible thing to do to a person."

Bexlee thought about all the conversations she'd had with Cyrus since they'd met. Would he want this? Would he take well to learning that the world was so much bigger than he'd ever imagined? Of anyone she'd ever met ...

"Yes."

"Then do it."

Bexlee looked up at Wynn. "I'm going to bite him. Hold him while I shift."

"You're going to *what?*"

She shook her head while she stripped. "No time. I just spoke to Tamsin. It's the only way to save him."

Wynn took over holding Cyrus, her jaw slack with wonder, as Bexlee let her wolf out. She urged the change to go faster than normal, and it hurt.

Once on four paws, she gazed at her partner. She could smell the acrid scent of his sweat and fear. She'd never done this. She didn't have time to dawdle. The theory was it had to be more than a small bite, otherwise every time a werewolf kissed someone it could lead to turning a person. But the bite couldn't be fatal. The wolf could heal a lot, but not death. She darted in and bit his belly and hip. She let her saliva mix with his blood.

He screamed in pain but didn't wake up.

It cut through her, making her whine. Wynn's gaze softened. "Change and wash up. I'll stay with him. We'll know soon enough if it worked."

When she returned from the bathroom, Cyrus's wounds were healing—he was healing. They took one of the cushions from a chair and placed it under his head.

Wynn gazed down at him. "How long do you think this will take?"

"I don't know. I've never done this before. I just ... I couldn't let him die. Not another one. Those damn black witches. They can't take everyone from us."

A low rumble came from the ground. "Wait, I was right? There are really witches?"

They knelt down next to him and helped him sit up. Bexlee rubbed his back. "How do you feel?"

His brow furrowed. "Good. But I had a nightmare that something tried to eat me." He patted his side. His fingers played with the holes in his clothes. "Did something try to eat me?"

With a sigh, Bexlee explained what happened. She knew he wouldn't believe everything, not at first. Wynn agreed to shift so Bexlee could continue explaining everything.

"Whoa, no reason to get naked to prove a point, I believe you, I believe you."

They both could smell the lie. "First rule," Bexlee said with a laugh. "You're going to have a lot of new senses. One will be the ability to smell lies. It's a blessing and a curse in our job. So, lying to us isn't going to work."

Once Wynn's fur and fangs appeared, Cyrus froze gaping. "Holy shit, you're not telling me a drunken tale? You're a fucking werewolf? They're fucking real? And you fucking bit me? Fucking hell, Court, why?" He spoke faster, his voice sounding more hysterical with every question.

"The sweet tea was spiked with the concoction. We didn't know. You were going to die. I'm sorry if I made the wrong decision. I just ... I didn't want you to die."

His focus shifted from the gray wolf, to Bexlee, to the jug of tea, then back to Bexlee. "Okay, yeah, I don't want to be dead." He raked his fingers through his hair. "A werewolf ... not a werebear?"

"I don't think there are werebears."

"Damn, that'd be really fucking cool. Okay, so, I'll turn into a wolf at the next full moon."

"Next week."

His eyes narrowed. "Right. You probably know the phases of the moon really well."

She smiled. "Yep, every month. It's something we all know."

"Werewolves. And witches? There are really witches?"

Bexlee took a deep breath; she hated having to dump so much on him. "Yes. Some good, some bad."

"Wicked witch of the west, got it. And that Loui guy, bad witch?"

"Bad witch; we call them black witches."

He leaned back on his hands and laughed. "And now that I know all this, I can't tell anyone, because they'll think I'm nuts. Fan-fucking-tastic. And the case is solved—but it isn't. No wonder you drink so much coffee." His head fell back, and he gazed at the clouds. "I *knew* it had to be witches!"

Find the Next Book
Pack Triage, here
mybook.to/PackTriage

Where to Find Harlowe Frost
Thanks for reading!
Find more of my books on my website:
http://hannahwillowauthor.com

You can also find me on:
Twitter: @hannahwillow217
Instagram: @hannahwillow217
Facebook Hannah Willow

Dedication:

Book four! We are half way through this series. I hope you're enjoying this as much as I enjoy creating the world and each story. I had a special writing group read through this one. They seemed to enjoy it. As always, Wes Imrisek and Angela Grimes help me get through the daily grind of writing, ensuring my story gets to you in it's best form!

About the Author

Harlowe Frost has been a teacher at both the high school and college level. Her parents instilled a love of reading from a young age. She grew up in the queer community. Her favorite genre growing up was fantasy and science fiction, that is, until she discovered urban fantasy and paranormal romance. What she never found in those books was the diversity in background, gender identity, and sexuality she saw in the people around her. She decided if she couldn't find that in what she read, then she would write it herself. This started her writing paranormal romance with a LGBTQ+ background

Made in United States
Troutdale, OR
11/27/2023

15044297R00159